"So if **skelet** **s**

Bethany's father sounded horrified.

"There are a lot of Jane Does out there," Bethany said. Her job for the past several years had been to discover who they were, and who their killers were, so they could get justice. But for some reason now it didn't seem as important to her as it once had; maybe because she knew there would always be more. She hadn't expected for one to show up here, though.

"That's sad," a deep voice murmured.

Bethany tensed before turning toward Cody. He'd slipped out of his truck and walked up without her noticing. Maybe it was good she was taking a break if she'd been that unaware of her surroundings, of a potential threat. Especially with all those other warnings she'd received.

Cody didn't pose a physical threat, but he unsettled her all the same. He threatened her peace of mind and her heart, just as he had all those years ago...

Ever since **Lisa Childs** read her first romance novel (a Harlequin story, of course) at age eleven, all she wanted was to be a romance writer. With over seventy novels published with Harlequin, Lisa is living her dream. She is an award-winning, bestselling romance author. She loves to hear from readers, who can contact her on Facebook or through her website, lisachilds.com.

Books by Lisa Childs

Harlequin Heartwarming

Bachelor Cowboys

A Rancher's Promise
The Cowboy's Unlikely Match
The Bronc Rider's Twin Surprise
The Cowboy's Ranch Rescue

Harlequin Romantic Suspense

Hotshot Heroes

Hotshot Hero Under Fire
Hotshot Hero on the Edge
Hotshot Heroes Under Threat

Visit the Author Profile page
at Harlequin.com for more titles.

BURIED
RANCH SECRETS

LISA CHILDS

LOVE INSPIRED
INSPIRATIONAL ROMANCE

LOVE INSPIRED®
INSPIRATIONAL ROMANCE

Recycling programs for this product may not exist in your area.

ISBN-13: 978-1-335-42613-0

Buried Ranch Secrets

Copyright © 2022 by Lisa Childs

For questions and comments about the quality of this book, please contact us at CustomerService@Harlequin.com.

Love Inspired
22 Adelaide St. West, 41st Floor
Toronto, Ontario M5H 4E3, Canada
www.LoveInspired.com

Printed in U.S.A.

For there is nothing covered, that shall not be revealed; neither hid, that shall not be known.
—*Luke* 12:2

For my kids—Ashley, Chloe, Brady and Carter—
for bringing so much love and joy to my life!

Chapter One

"Daddy, where are the bears?" Molly asked the question she'd been asking since Cody Shepard had moved his daughter to his hometown of Bear Creek, Montana, a few months ago. From her booster carseat, the four-year-old could easily see out the passenger's window of the pickup truck. The truck had no back seat, but that was fine. It was just the two of them most of the time. "I see the creek," she said as the truck tires rumbled across the bridge, "but there are never any bears in it."

Her bottom lip pulled into a slight pout, and when she turned toward him, her green eyes were narrowed with suspicion, like she thought he'd lied to her about the name. As the tires hit each rut in the old ranch road, her strawberry blond curls bounced around the shoulders of her fake-fur zebra-print coat. She looked a lot like him—though his hair was a dark blond now and not nearly as curly as it had once been, probably because he kept it short. Their eyes were the same, though—even the suspicion. Cody struggled to trust anyone.

"Am I ever gonna see a bear?" she asked, her voice

weary beyond her young years. She was also so smart and mature beyond her years and so very dramatic.

Cody's lips curved into the smile his little girl always managed to pull out of him, even when he was about as stressed as he could be. And he was plenty stressed right now when trying to excavate for the new barn before the ground froze too hard for them to dig the footings.

Even now snowflakes drifted down outside the warm cab of the pickup truck. At least they were thick and wet and melted when they hit the ground. He'd gotten lucky that they hadn't had a hard freeze yet, especially this late in the year. Setback after setback had happened though, pushing back the excavator's arrival until after Thanksgiving.

Cody sped across the ranch property, toward the site where he used to speed on horseback so many years ago, to meet someone else. But he pushed thoughts of *her* from his mind, as he always had these past twelve years, and he focused all his attention and his love on his daughter.

"I'm sorry, sweetheart," he said, addressing her disappointment. "But there are definitely bears here. You just haven't seen one yet." And he kind of hoped she never did, at least not up close. He didn't want her to get hurt any more than she had been. She'd suffered disappointment too many times already in her young life, and not just over not seeing bears. Now she no longer saw her mother, not that she'd seen much of her before Theresa had terminated her parental rights.

"Maybe I'll ask Santa to bring me a bear for Christmas," she said.

He grimaced. "That probably wouldn't be a good idea,

sweetheart. We wouldn't want the bear to hurt Snowball."

Her green eyes widened with horror. "A bear would hurt my kitty?"

He shrugged. "I don't know, but it would be better not to take any chances, don't you think?"

She emitted a soft little sigh and nodded. "You're right."

He hoped she always agreed with him so easily. But she was only four—four and a half as she often reminded him. They had a lot of years ahead of them—just the two of them. He reached across the console and stroked his hand over her silky hair. "What else are you going to ask Santa for?" he asked.

He had some time before he needed to worry about his Christmas shopping, but with as busy as he was, it would be better to start now so that he could find what she wanted while the stores were fully stocked.

"I dunno…" she mumbled, and she turned back to peer out the passenger window as if she couldn't meet his gaze.

Was there something his daughter wanted that she didn't want to tell him about? Something that she was worried would hurt his feelings?

Like a mother?

"Oh, baby…" he murmured. "You know you can tell me anything."

"I'll tell Santa," she said. "He'll bring it for me."

If she wanted her mother, Santa wasn't going to be able to bring Theresa back. Theresa had moved on without a second thought about their daughter or about him.

Cody was used to that. His mother had done the same

to him and his father; she'd left them without ever looking back, without ever contacting them again. And then Bethany—beautiful Bethany Snow—had done the same thing to him, breaking his teenage heart right here.

That was why he'd been so careful when he'd gotten married. He'd proposed more out of friendship than love, thinking he and Theresa had the same goals and values. And maybe they'd had, but when they'd had Molly, his goals and values had changed. He'd fallen in love far deeper than he'd ever had before...deeper even than with Bethany Snow.

He loved his daughter so much there was no sacrifice he wouldn't make for her well-being, for her happiness. "I want to get you something for Christmas, too," he told her. "So you need to let me in on your secret with Santa."

She turned back to him, those green eyes narrowed with suspicion. "But what if Santa thinks you're going to get it for me and you don't, and then I don't get it at all?"

"So there is something?" he asked.

She shrugged again. "I dunno..."

A pang of panic struck his heart. Molly always told him everything—all the time. She chattered on and on about her friends from preschool and about her teacher and all the other people who worked at the church school. She even told him all about the antics of her dolls and of course her kitty, Snowball. Why was she clamming up now?

That pang left an ache in his heart that had him reaching up to rub his chest. Worrying about her was something he always did, probably always would do, but he would have to deal with those worries a little later, when he had time to focus only on her.

He wondered if he would ever have that time with all the responsibility for the ranch falling on him now. As well as the new barn, there were cattle to tend, feed to grow and ranch hands to direct. But that was good; then he could secure the ranch for Molly's future.

"Look, Daddy! Look at the big Tonka trucks!" Molly exclaimed, as she peered now through the windshield at where the excavator had parked his dump truck and bulldozer.

Finally. Bruce Willard was here. But those Tonka trucks weren't moving. The man and a couple of his workers were standing around instead, staring down into a hole.

Cody suppressed a groan. It was a good thing he'd come out to check on them. He'd just intended to make sure that the measurements were big enough for the barn he was building to expand the Shepard Ranch into boarding and breeding horses. This area was closer to the main road leading back to Bear Creek and farther from the ranch house and buildings. Halfway between the ranch and the town, between him and her.

But that had been years ago. There was much more than space between him and Bethany Snow now. There were years and years. He'd pushed aside all thoughts of the past when he'd chosen this site for the new barn. He'd considered only that it was closer to town and farther from Cody's father so that the construction didn't upset him. There was also a well on the property since there had once been a house here, too, years ago.

Cody parked his truck near the dump truck. "I'll be right back," he told Molly, who was already fumbling with the seat belt that wound through her booster seat.

He used to call her Houdini for how quickly she'd figured out how to unbuckle her car seats. But he'd made certain she knew to never do it while the vehicle was moving.

"But I wanna ride the big Tonka truck, Daddy," she said.

"It's not running right now," he pointed out. "So let me talk to the guys who drive those and find out what's going on." Bruce Willard didn't monitor his speech in the presence of children, and Cody didn't want his daughter learning any new and inappropriate words from the excavator. "I'll be right back," he assured her again.

Then he stepped out of the truck and approached the workers. Bruce turned toward him and said, "I was just getting ready to call you."

"Is there a problem?" Cody asked, but he knew there must have been if the excavator had been about to contact him. "Is the ground too frozen?"

They'd already moved a big mound of dirt, though, and they were all standing around a hole. A shiver raced down Cody's spine as he walked up to join them. Maybe one of those fat snowflakes had slipped between the rim of his hat and the sheepskin collar of his coat. Or maybe he knew this was going to be another problem, one bigger than the ground being frozen.

Bruce shook his head. "No," he groaned. "But I sure do wish it was because then we wouldn't have found that." He extended a shaking hand toward the hole.

Cody stepped closer to peer over the edge and down at the dirt-encrusted bones of a skeleton. He shuddered then quickly glanced back at the pickup to make sure

Molly hadn't wriggled down from her booster seat to check out those Tonka trucks. She waved at him through the windshield, and he waved back, and now his own hand was shaking a little. He sure didn't want her to see this; he wished now that *he* hadn't.

"What do you think?" Cody asked. "Did we disturb an old graveyard?" Sometimes settlers had buried their dead near their homes.

Bruce shook his head again. "There was no stone or anything marking it. I don't think anybody else knows this body was here but the killer."

Cody gasped. "Killer? What are you talking about?"

"Look at the skull," Bruce said. "Our machine didn't do that…"

Cody leaned over to peer closer at the skeleton and noticed the cracks on the skull. "Are you sure?" he asked. "The machine didn't…"

"I didn't get that close to it," Bruce said. "I hit that first." He pointed toward a mound of dirt and the dented and rusted barrel sitting atop it. "And the body fell out of it." The older man shuddered now. "That's no casket, Cody. This wasn't any official grave we disturbed."

"No," Cody agreed. It wasn't. It was a crime scene. He'd already considered this spot a crime scene since having his heart broken here. But this was far more serious than a broken heart. This was murder.

"You better call the sheriff," Bruce said.

Cody was already reaching for his cell. This was bad for so many reasons. Someone had lost their life. That someone deserved to be identified and their killer brought to justice. That was all that really mattered. That was all Cody could focus on right now, but he had that niggling feeling again that he shouldn't have come home. And yet he'd been worried something bad would happen if he didn't. That body had probably been there longer than the three months since his return, though. Maybe even years...

It had been years since Bethany Snow had come home for Christmas. She'd always claimed in the past that she'd been too busy to make the trip from Chicago to Bear Creek. The truth was she just hadn't wanted to come home.

She wasn't sure she wanted to return even now, but she'd run out of excuses. And, if she accepted that new position in New York, she probably wouldn't have the time to visit again for many more years.

"This is all you've brought?" her dad asked as he reached for the carry-on bag she held. "I thought you were staying until Christmas."

She had the time off—vacation and personal days she had to use before the end of the year or she would lose them. She just wasn't sure she wanted to spend all those days in Bear Creek.

While her mother had visited her in Chicago over the years, Bethany hadn't seen much of her father since she'd left for college. Of course, she'd never seen much of him before she'd left either. She stopped now to study him as he stood on the sidewalk outside the airport, waiting for her to hand over the bag.

While he still stood straight and tall with the posture of the army officer he had been for so many years, he'd aged. He wasn't as broad, as muscular, and there were more lines in his face, his skin pale beneath the brim of his hat as if he hadn't been outside as much as he used to be. He looked older than his sixty-five years, but his blue eyes were as sharp as ever. "We're holding up traffic, Beth," he said. "You got something in that bag you need?"

She shook her head and passed it over to him. He opened the back door and tossed it onto the seat of the SUV. Then, ever the gentleman, he opened the front passenger door for her. When she started toward it, he closed his arms around her and pulled her into a tight embrace.

Unused to affection from him, she stiffened for a moment with surprise before she closed her arms around him and hugged him. And some of the tension eased from her body as warmth flooded her heart. He'd never been *Daddy* to her. He'd always been *Sir* and *Father*. Someone she respected and obeyed, not someone she hugged. But she hugged him now before she remembered this wasn't what they did and pulled back. "I'm surprised you came and not Mom," she admitted.

He sighed. "I'm sorry, Beth."

She wasn't sure what he was apologizing for, and she stiffened again with sudden alarm. "Is Mom okay?" she asked. "Has something happened to her?"

"No, of course not," he said, and he shook his head. "I just…well, we'll talk about that later. Your mother's busy at the church."

Bethany smiled. "Of course she is." Her mother was the ultimate church lady, serving on every committee while helping out every member. "She should have been a minister herself." She probably would have been— a minister or a teacher—had she not married a military man and given up her own dreams to follow him around the world.

A horn tooted behind them, startling Bethany again. Her father was right—they were holding up traffic. He lifted his hand to wave as he walked around to the driver's side of the SUV. Bethany settled onto the passenger's seat and pulled the door closed just as he pulled away from the curb. He'd aged, but he still moved fast.

"I'm surprised you weren't too busy to come," she said.

He glanced across the console at her. "It's Bear Creek," he said. "Nothing much happening..."

That had never stopped him before from being too busy to come to her school conferences or choir concerts. Then, he'd always found something that had been more important than her.

Some crime.

Some disorderly conduct.

Once he'd retired from the military, her father had been elected sheriff of Bear Creek—the town where he and her mother had grown up, where they'd met and married before traveling all around the world. And after traveling all around the world, of all the other places they'd lived, they'd decided to come back and live in Bear Creek.

"That's good though," her father said. "Good that it's quiet and safe, especially right now."

She tensed again, wondering what he was talking about. Her? Did he think she needed a break? He wasn't wrong, but how did he know when she was reluctant to admit it even to herself? That maybe it had all been too much…

"Why right now?" she asked.

"It's Christmastime, Beth," he said. "Good to enjoy Christmas."

She nodded.

"You haven't done that," he said. "You've always been too busy working."

She wanted to call him on his hypocrisy. But, despite the hug, he was still *Sir* and *Father* to her. So she bit her bottom lip.

He reached across the console and squeezed her arm. "It's so good to have you home, Beth."

She wanted to say that it was good to be home, but she wasn't sure that Bear Creek was home. Sure, the four years she'd lived there during high school was the most of her childhood that she'd spent in any one place, but that didn't make it home. Bethany wasn't certain that she'd ever felt at home in any place.

Now, with a person…

She drew in a quick breath, but she shouldn't have been surprised that she would think of Cody Shepard. She was in Bear Creek, or they would be in the little less than an hour it would take to get there from the airport.

But Cody wasn't in Bear Creek; he'd left when she had. And she doubted he'd been back even the couple of times that she'd visited since high school. He'd been even less connected to his family than she'd been to hers.

"So why the small bag?" her father persisted. "Why didn't you pack more?"

He was smart; he probably suspected she didn't intend to stay long.

"Christmas is three weeks away," he said. "You're going to need more stuff."

She nodded. "If I do, I'll go shopping," she said.

"Your mother would love to go with you," he said, his deep voice warming with affection for his wife.

Bethany smiled. "Yes, she will." She hadn't often agreed to go shopping with her mother; she'd been so determined to be exactly the opposite of the girly homemaker her mother had wanted her to be, that her mother was.

Good thing Bethany had not been an only child, just the youngest. Her older sister, Diana, was their mother's clone and not just because she'd inherited her red hair and green eyes, whereas Bethany had their father's black hair and blue eyes. Diana was exactly like her mother in personality and lifestyle, right down to marrying a military man and raising her young family on army bases all over the world. They weren't going to make it back from Germany this year. Neither was Bethany's brother, Bill. He was the minister their mother probably should have been, and he and his family couldn't get away from the new church where he'd just been assigned in Boston.

"It's probably going to be a hard Christmas for Mom," Bethany said, "with the grandchildren not being here for her to spoil."

Her father glanced at her, and he was grinning. "Is that why you finally agreed to come home for Christmas? You knew there'd be no kids underfoot?"

She was surprised he was teasing her and surprised he was so astute. She chuckled. "Maybe…"

The few times she'd visited her brother or her sister, the chaos had overwhelmed her. And Bethany was used to chaos; she just wasn't used to children. If she accepted this new position, she wouldn't have the chance to get used to them. She'd be much too busy to visit her family or to have one of her own.

Not that she wanted one.

She'd decided long ago that she wanted to focus on a career. And she'd given up her love…

"Sheriff?" A voice emanated from the radio on the dash of the SUV. "Are you available, Sheriff?"

He sighed and picked up the receiver. "Gerty," he said into the speaker, "don't you remember I'm picking up my daughter from the airport?"

"Yes, sir," Gerty replied. "But there's kind of an emergency."

"Kind of?" he asked. "Has there been an accident?"

"They don't think it was an accident," Gerty said, "but a body's been found."

Her father gasped. "A body? Where?"

"The Shepard Ranch, sir," Gerty replied.

Bethany's stomach flipped.

"Do you want me to send someone else?" Gerty asked.

"Is there any chance of this person surviving?" her father asked.

"It's too late for that, sir," Gerty said. "What they found was a skeleton."

"Then there's no rush to send someone else," her father said. "I'll come out when I get back." He glanced over at Bethany. "Actually we'll head straight there. Tell them we're about forty-five minutes away." He clicked off the radio then.

"We'll head straight there?" Bethany asked. "What is this? Bring your daughter to work day?" A pang of longing struck her heart over all the times she'd implored him to do just that, to let her tag along with him, but he hadn't thought it was appropriate back then. He hadn't wanted her to get hurt or to witness anything unsavory.

He wouldn't believe all the horrible things she'd seen since then. And despite his best efforts to protect her, she had been hurt in Bear Creek. Just not physically...

"It is when my daughter has a whole lot more experience with murder investigations than I do, Special Agent Snow."

"Murder?" she repeated. "You think it's a murder?"

"You heard Gerty. She said they didn't think it was an accident. But you'll be better able to determine that than anyone else in Bear Creek, Beth. You're the FBI agent." Her father actually sounded proud of that, proud of her.

That was all she'd ever wanted from him—some of the respect she'd always had for him. But she couldn't take even a moment to savor it. One, because a body had been discovered. And two, because that body had been discovered at the Shepard Ranch.

Going out there again shouldn't be a problem, though. It wasn't like Cody was home. He'd sworn that once he left Bear Creek he was never coming back.

Then, of course, she'd sworn the same thing herself—and here she was.

Chapter Two

"Daddy, look at the pretty lights!" Molly exclaimed as she peered out the front windows of the farmhouse on the Shepard Ranch. She wasn't referring to Christmas lights. Cody hadn't had time to put those up yet, and now he wasn't sure when he would have time. "But they're so loud!" She covered her ears and scrunched her cute face into a grimace.

Cody flinched, at the noise, and at the sheriff's arrival to the ranch. Why had Mike Snow used the lights and sirens? Cody glanced over his shoulder at the hall leading to his father's room at the back of the sprawling ranch house. Had he heard them?

Cody hadn't told Don Shepard yet what had been found on the property. He wasn't sure he wanted to tell him. It would only add to the older man's confusion and then his frustration. That frustration gnawed at Cody as well. It was so hard to see his father, a man who'd always been so stoic and strong, like *this*, to see him so helpless.

It made Cody feel helpless, too. Just like he felt now.

He was also confused. He had no idea to whom that skeleton could belong. He doubted it had been put there while he'd been living on the ranch. He'd spent so much time out at the site of that old homestead he would have noticed if the ground had been disturbed. It must have been buried there sometime after he'd left. He'd been gone a long time. He had no idea who might have gone missing from town over the past twelve years, or maybe it had been someone just passing through who had wound up staying in Bear Creek against their will.

Sometimes Cody felt like that, like it was how he'd come back—against his will. But he also believed it would be for the best for Molly to stop traveling and to settle in one place, and it was especially best for his father. Cody wasn't sure about himself yet. Since becoming a father, he'd learned to worry about himself last.

"Sheriff Snow is here to talk to me about that work being done on the ranch," Cody told his daughter, which was partially the truth since the body had been discovered while digging those footings for the new barn. "It's going to be boring for you to listen to, so you should go up to your room and play with your dolls or with Snowball."

The little girl glanced around the living room. "Where did Snowball go?"

"The siren probably scared her," Cody said. "You should make sure she's okay."

His little girl nodded, but before she could head up the stairs to her room, the doorbell rang. They didn't get much company on the ranch, so Molly was always very interested in visitors, too interested usually. She rushed across the living room to the foyer and pulled open the front door.

"You scared my kitty," he heard her tell the sheriff, who hadn't stepped inside yet. Then Molly said, "I didn't know the sheriff's a lady."

Cody's brow furrowed with confusion until he realized that the Bear Creek Police Department might have a female deputy on staff now. Fortunately Cody hadn't had any interactions with the police since he'd moved back to Bear Creek. He wished he wasn't having this one either, but at least Mike Snow hadn't showed up. Seeing him would summon all Cody's memories of the man's daughter. That was why Cody hadn't rushed right to the door; he needed a moment to deal with those memories.

Before Cody could join his daughter and the deputy in the foyer, he heard a familiar voice say, "I'm not the sheriff, and I'm sorry we scared your kitty."

"Who are you?" Molly asked.

Cody knew—he would have recognized that voice anywhere. He still heard it so often in his dreams, even more so lately since she'd been on the news, giving interviews about all those open cases she'd recently closed. And just as the sound of her voice had affected him then, it affected him now, making his stomach twist into knots.

"I'm Agent Snow," Bethany replied. "This is the sheriff. He's also my dad."

"Your daddy is the sheriff?" Molly asked with awe in her suddenly soft voice.

Cody wasn't sure why that would impress her so much. Did she even know what a sheriff was? But maybe she'd heard other people—at preschool or church—talk about the sheriff. The former army colonel had earned the respect of everyone in town; it was why nobody ever ran against him for sheriff.

"Then Mrs. Snow is your mommy?" she asked, and now she sounded even more impressed.

While Bethany emitted a soft gasp of surprise, her dad chuckled. "Yes, she is," he answered for her. "And now may we speak with your daddy, honey?"

"Who's her daddy?" Bethany asked her father.

Cody forced himself to cross the last few feet of the living room to join them in the foyer. Even though he'd seen her recently on the news, nothing had prepared him for seeing her in person again. She was so beautiful with her pale ivory skin and that gleaming black hair that seemed to reflect highlights the same startling blue as her eyes.

"I'm her daddy," Cody replied with pride, and he boosted his daughter onto his hip. Then he greeted his visitor. "Hello, Bethany."

Her scarf loosened around her long neck as she swallowed then nodded. "Hello, Cody…"

"You know my daddy?" Molly asked.

Bethany nodded. "Yes, we went to school together a long time ago."

"Like me and Owen Moore?"

"I don't know Owen Moore," Bethany replied.

"He's a boy in my preschool class," she replied, and her face scrunched into a grimace again. "He says he's going to marry me someday."

Cody gasped now. "I might need to have a talk with Owen."

Bethany's dad chuckled again. "I remember having that talk myself with a certain young man…" He held out his hand. "Good to see you, Cody."

Cody shook the sheriff's hand with his free one. "You, too, sir. Just wish it was under different circumstances."

"We're here now to investigate these *circumstances*," the sheriff said.

"We?" Cody asked with a glance at Bethany.

He couldn't look at her for more than a glance, or he was likely to find himself staring with his mouth open, like he used to when they'd been in school together. But that had been high school, not preschool. He really needed to have a talk with Owen.

While Cody couldn't meet Bethany's eyes, he found himself glancing at her hands…to see if anyone had ever convinced her to marry him. But in deference to the weather, she wore gloves that were so thick he couldn't tell if there was a wedding band or an engagement ring beneath them.

"You must have heard about Beth's work as an FBI agent since she's been all over the news," her father said with obvious pride in his daughter. "She's better equipped to handle this investigation than I am, especially since it sounds like a cold case."

"If you're cold, come inside," Molly said, misinterpreting what they were saying—which was a good thing.

Cody didn't want her to know what had been found on the ranch. He wished he didn't know, that he could unsee what he'd seen.

"Honey, that's really sweet of you to invite us in, but we can't stay," the sheriff told Molly. Then he focused on Cody again. "We need to get started on the investigation. I was picking up Beth from the airport when Gerty put out the radio call about what you'd found out here."

"That's why she said it would be a while," Cody said. He'd wondered why the sheriff wouldn't have sent someone out right away with a body being found under such strange circumstances. He wished the dispatcher had told him why it would take so long and had warned him about Bethany so that he could have braced himself.

So that he wouldn't have been taken so by surprise that his head felt a little light, his knees a little weak. Or maybe that was just his delayed reaction to seeing that skeleton, to knowing that someone had died—or at the very least been buried—on the ranch.

"It gets dark earlier this time of year," the sheriff continued to prod, "so we really need to get out there now."

Cody nodded. "I understand. Just let me make sure that somebody's around to watch Molly for me," he said.

"Molly," Bethany murmured as she stared at his daughter.

"I'm Molly," the little girl said with a smile for their visitor. Then she sent him a pointed look and proudly told him, "I can watch myself, Daddy. I'm a big girl. I'm almost five."

His lips curved into a slight smile at the thought that often crossed his mind about his fiercely independent daughter: she was four going on fourteen. "I know. But you can't take care of Snowball and Grandpa all by yourself. I have to make sure Sammy is back from the store."

"Sammy?" Bethany repeated that name, too. "Is that your wife?"

Molly giggled. "Sammy is a boy. And Daddy doesn't have a wife, and I don't have a mommy anymore."

Cody flinched at how matter of fact his daughter sounded over his divorce, over her mother cutting them both out of her life. He would make certain to never put himself, and especially Molly, through that kind of pain again. Neither of them could fall for someone who would leave them so easily.

"I'm sorry," Bethany said, her pale skin suddenly flushing with bright pink color. "I didn't know. I'm really sorry, Cody."

His face heated now as he realized she was offering him condolences he didn't deserve. From what Molly had said, Bethany must have misconstrued that his wife had died. That was pretty much how Molly had made it sound. Maybe that was how it felt to Molly. That final. That was how Theresa had made it sound to him, but he'd hoped Molly hadn't overheard or understood any of Theresa's reasoning for cutting herself out of their lives.

It's easier this way, Cody.

But it had only been easier for her. He shook his head. "That's not what…that's not…"

He didn't know how to explain it, especially within earshot of his daughter. Even if Molly hadn't been present, Cody wasn't sure he could have explained how everything had gone so wrong. He hadn't figured it out yet himself.

"There's Sammy!" Molly exclaimed, and she wriggled down from Cody's arms to run to the older man. In his midsixties, the bull fighter had been more than ready to retire from the rodeo, but Cody wondered if Sammy would have kept working if not for him and

Molly. Sammy had retired to come home with Cody and help him raise his daughter.

Sammy, with his long white hair and many scars and tattoos, didn't look much like the stereotypical Mary Poppins–kind of nanny. But since the day she'd been born, Molly had the old rodeo clown wrapped around her little finger.

Sammy grinned at her, a grin that exposed a few gold teeth and a couple of missing ones. "Hey there, Princess Molly," the old man greeted her as he swung the little girl up in his arms.

"I'm not a princess," she protested. Then, clasped yet in Sammy's strong arms, she turned toward Bethany. "*You* look like a princess," she said. "You're so very pretty."

Even as a teenager, Bethany had always been more than pretty. With that creamy skin and dark hair and those arresting blue eyes, she'd been stunning. And every time Cody had looked at her, he'd felt like he'd gotten thrown off a bronc and was flying through the air. Falling…

So hard for her.

As an adult, Bethany was even more stunning. Gorgeous.

"You look like Snow White," his daughter persisted, and her mouth dropped open with shock. "*Are* you Snow White?"

Bethany's lips curved into a slight smile now, and she shook her head. "No, I'm definitely not a princess."

"But you said your name is Agent Snow."

"Agent?" Sammy, his voice a little sharp with what was probably alarm, repeated the title, and he glanced from the little girl to their visitors standing on the porch.

Cody nodded. "Yes, Sammy Felton, this is FBI agent Bethany Snow and her dad, Sheriff Mike Snow. They've come to investigate that…*thing*… I told you the excavators found this afternoon." Though he could understand Sammy questioning a federal agent getting involved so soon in an investigation of some old bones. "Can you keep an eye on Dad and the little princess for me while I bring them out to the site?"

"You don't need to go with us right now," Bethany said. "Just tell us where it is that you made that discovery."

He braced himself then, even as his stomach muscles knotted tighter, and met her blue-eyed gaze. "The old homestead property near the main highway."

It was halfway between the ranch and the town. Halfway between his house and hers, where they used to meet so many years ago.

Because he was staring at her so intently, he saw her beautiful blue eyes darken to deep navy, and it was almost as if he could see the memories passing through her mind. The memories that passed through his now, of long moments talking and kissing and promising and planning a future that they had never shared.

All those promises of unending love had been just as empty as every other promise anyone had ever made Cody. Bethany had left him just like every other person in his life had except for his dad. Cody was the one who'd left his dad, disappointing him when he hadn't stayed to help out on the ranch. Guilt churned inside him that he'd stayed away so long, that he hadn't known how his dad had been struggling.

Cody had had to come home—for his dad. Why was Bethany back now? Just for Christmas and a cold case?

He doubted she was staying, especially with as high-profile as her career successes had become. She hadn't been able to wait to leave Bear Creek. Neither had he. Both had sworn they would never come back once they left.

He'd changed his mind about that when his circumstances had changed, when he'd become a single father and when his father had suddenly needed him. He doubted Bethany would ever change her mind about moving back. From what he could tell, the only thing she'd ever changed her mind about was loving him.

Bethany's pulse continued to race even after she closed the passenger's door on the SUV, even after she turned fully away from that ranch house and from Cody and his young daughter. Once her dad crawled into the driver's seat, she turned to him and said, "You could have warned me."

"Warned you?" he asked, and he sounded innocent enough—maybe even oblivious—but he didn't look at her. "About what?"

Had he been that unaware back then or maybe he just hadn't been interested in her teenage life? Had he not known how she and Cody had felt about each other? How serious they'd been? He'd made that comment to Cody about having had to talk to a boy about his daughter. Had he been talking about her? Or had he been talking about Diana's high school boyfriend who she'd married and followed around military bases?

She sighed. "You could have warned me about Cody. I didn't know he was home."

Her father shrugged. "He just moved back a few months ago."

"With a daughter," she said.

"Cute little thing," he said. "Your mother talks about her all the time, has a lot of fun with her in Sunday school and preschool."

Her mother probably knew every child in Bear Creek. "Mom never mentioned her to me," Bethany said, and she felt even more betrayed. Her mother had lived for her kids, so she'd known every detail about their lives. She'd known every detail about every one of their friends' lives, too. So she'd definitely known about Cody.

And she hadn't shared anything with Bethany, any information about his current situation. About his return to Bear Creek with his daughter.

Her heart pounded so hard that she wanted to reach up and press her hand against it, but she wouldn't reveal to her father—or even to herself—just how much seeing Cody again had affected her. It was like that first time she'd seen him in the hall at school, that moment their gazes had locked and she'd felt like for the first time ever that someone really saw *her*. Not just the new kid or the sheriff's daughter or the church lady's kid…

Her.

Bethany.

And she'd seen him, too, had seen that he wasn't as carefree and happy as he pretended he was. She'd seen the pain he'd been hiding, the ambition, the dreams. She'd seen all that in his deep green eyes, just as he'd seen everything in hers.

"I'm sure your mother would have told you if she thought it would matter to you. But you've been so busy with your important work, with closing all those old cases from that serial killer you caught," her father said, and there was that pride in his voice again, that pride she'd heard earlier.

That pride that had warmth flooding her heart. Was that what it had taken for her father to finally notice her? To finally respect her? All the media attention over her catching a serial killer?

She'd solved other cases since she'd joined the FBI, even when she'd just started as a forensics analyst. She'd worked hard to earn the respect of her colleagues, to earn the promotion she'd been offered. But none of that mattered as much to her as this, as hearing that pride in her father's voice. Tears stung her eyes, but she blinked them back, determined to be the professional he finally believed she was.

He reached across the console and squeezed her arm like he had earlier, with an easy affection she didn't remember him ever doling out before. "I'm so glad you're home," he said. "For Christmas and for this case."

"I'm sure you could handle this investigation on your own, Dad," she assured him. She was so certain he could that she was surprised by how insistent he'd been about turning it over to her. On their way to the ranch, they'd made some calls—one to City Hall to talk to the mayor and another to her boss at the bureau office in Chicago. Both of them had agreed that she could work the case.

Her boss had been amused that Bethany had only been off work for a few hours before finding a new case. And the mayor had been grateful that she would even consider investigating their small-town situation. Her father, though, was the most relieved.

And she wondered...

"Is everything all right, Dad?" she asked.

"Yes, of course," he said. "You know Bear Creek. It's a quiet town. Nothing much ever happens here. The only people that die, who haven't died of old age or illness, die in traffic accidents or ranch accidents. In a couple of those cases, other people have been negligent for those accidents, because of drunkenness or recklessness, and I had to arrest them. But I haven't had an actual *murder* to investigate since I became sheriff sixteen years ago."

A sigh of relief escaped Bethany's lips at the realization that there was one place where murders didn't routinely happen, where people didn't purposely and callously take the lives of others. Maybe that was part of the reason she'd decided to come home this Christmas; she'd needed a break from all the horrors with which she'd been dealing.

She'd figured that here in Bear Creek she would find respite from all that evil. Apparently she'd been wrong.

Even *here* something bad had happened.

Cody Shepard had found a body on his ranch. No, not just on his ranch, but at their place—the special spot where they'd met so many times to discuss their dreams for their future, a future they'd foolishly figured they could share no matter if they'd wanted completely different things out of life.

He'd wanted to join the rodeo, to travel the country while riding for championship belts. And she'd wanted to go to college and follow her father's footsteps into law enforcement. She'd realized, before Cody had, that there was no way they could both achieve their dreams if they tried to achieve them together. She hadn't wanted to be like her mother; she hadn't wanted to follow a man around the world, living his dreams while letting her own die. But she hadn't wanted Cody to sacrifice his dreams for hers either; she'd loved him too much.

She'd loved him so much she'd broken up with him at their special spot so many years ago. Maybe it was fitting that it was a crime scene now. That person— whoever they were—hadn't been the only thing to die there; their love had, too. But Bethany was the one who'd killed that.

She doubted it would have survived if she hadn't. And she'd wanted to end it quickly and cleanly instead of dragging it out and making both of them miserable.

Chapter Three

Cody didn't have to return to the scene. Bethany had assured him of that before she and her father had walked down the steps from the porch to the sheriff's SUV. She'd said that if she had any questions for him that she would come back to the house.

But Cody didn't want her coming back to the house. He didn't want to talk to her where Molly or his father might overhear them. So, after making sure Sammy had everything under control, Cody had hopped into his truck again to head back out to the spot.

Their spot...

It hadn't been that for a dozen years, though. "They" hadn't been for a dozen years. But for those four years she'd lived in Bear Creek, she'd been everything to him. His best friend, the love of his life, his soul mate, or so he'd thought.

Then she'd set him straight—the night of their high school graduation. After their parties, she had asked him to meet her at their spot and then she'd told him that they had nothing in common and that they had no future. She hadn't known about the engagement ring in his pocket, the one he'd worked hard to save for, the one he'd intended to propose with that very night.

While she was all he'd ever wanted, she'd told him that she wanted much more out of life than him. He'd felt a sharp jab to his heart then, so painful that he'd nearly doubled over from it. Even now, all these years later, there was still a dull ache in his chest from that heartbreak—though it hadn't been his first or his last.

He hadn't argued with her then because he'd known she was right, that she was smarter than him, more driven, and she deserved so much more in life than what he would ever be able to offer her. So he'd kept the ring in his pocket and he hadn't stopped her when she'd walked away and driven off.

From the recent interviews lauding her success at finding a serial killer, for solving all the murders the man had committed over the years, she'd found much more in life than Cody. She had the career and the re-spect she'd always wanted.

He was happy for her. And no matter how crazy his life was, he was happy for himself, too. He had won most, if not all, of the championship belts he'd wanted to win. He'd even landed a couple of the endorsements and contracts of his teenage dreams, and he'd invested that money wisely because he'd known that a rodeo ca-reer didn't last long. At least not as a rider. And once a rider wasn't riding anymore, they were quickly forgot-ten. But Cody had something better than the fame and fortune his teenage self had craved: he had his daughter.

And that made him feel incredibly blessed no matter

what else was going on with his dad or with the ranch. He had Molly, and she was *everything* to him.

Just like Bethany Snow had once been.

When Cody neared the site, he noticed that the sheriff's SUV wasn't the only vehicle parked near the heavy equipment that had uncovered the body. Two vans had pulled up near the SUV. One probably belonged to the coroner and maybe the other belonged to the state police or even the FBI—though Cody wasn't sure where the FBI office was in Montana. There certainly wasn't one in Bear Creek. So Bethany wasn't here to work.

She had to have just come home for a visit. With as desperate as she'd been to leave this place in her teens, there was no way she was staying in Bear Creek any longer than she had to. There was nothing to keep her here for longer than the holidays except for this case her father had enlisted her to investigate.

Bethany could feel him watching her. Cody hadn't stepped out of the pickup truck that he'd driven up in a while ago, but she was very aware of his presence in that parked vehicle. Taller and more muscular than he'd been at eighteen, he had even more presence than he'd had as a teenager. And he'd actually had quite the presence then. Everybody had always been aware of him—of who he was, of what he could be. He'd had that *it* potential.

Every boy had wanted to be like him. Every girl had wanted to be *with* him. Everyone had just known he was going to be somebody someday.

Famous.

He had been for a while. At least when she'd paid attention to the rodeo news, to when she'd watched the televised competitions and had seen him win. He'd been the champion he'd always wanted to be while she'd been working hard on her degree, finishing school and not missing him so much that she wanted to quit it all and track him down wherever he was. But then she'd remember her mother's life, how much she'd sacrificed for her husband. How she'd sacrificed herself.

She swallowed the sigh burning the back of her throat. It wasn't of self-pity, though. She hadn't really wanted to get married, and she didn't want a family. She wanted exactly what she had: her career, which was going better than she could have imagined. At thirty, she could become the leader of her own FBI cold case unit in one of the biggest cities…if she accepted that promotion. Why hadn't she accepted it yet?

Why had she said she needed to think about it? Was she letting those letters, those threats, get to her? Serial killers often had fans, people who rooted for them and resented the agents who'd brought them to justice. She knew better than to take it personally, than to be afraid of some empty threats. That had nothing to do with her hesitation in accepting that promotion.

Maybe she'd just needed some time off to relax and recharge here at home. But instead she was working another cold case. From the condition of the remains, this body had been buried here for a while, so this case was probably even colder than the ones she'd recently closed. She turned away from that truck where Cody sat, watching her through the windshield, and she focused on the crime scene again. Maybe the crime hadn't happened here. Maybe the body had only been dumped here, buried where the killer had probably never expected anyone to discover it.

To discover *her*…

From the small stature of the bones, from the width and curvature of the pelvis, Bethany was pretty certain that the victim had been a woman. One who'd probably borne a child.

Molly had said her mother was gone, and Bethany had assumed that meant she was dead. Was she? And had she been properly buried somewhere or…?

Bethany needed to question Cody, needed to determine what he knew about these bones—if he knew the person to whom they belonged. But first she focused on getting the scene properly documented before releasing the bones, and the barrel in which they'd been buried, to the state police lab. They would be able to determine how long ago this person had died, how long they'd been buried here.

Bethany could already tell how she'd died. From a violent blow to the head.

Probably from a hammer or some other tool. With as much damage as that blow had caused to the skull, this hadn't been an accidental death. It was murder. One someone had tried to cover up by burying her in that old barrel. It smelled faintly of gasoline and had probably once had some type of nozzle on top to distribute the gas it had carried.

For the ranch? Had it been used here? Or somewhere else and just dumped here with the body? After directing the techs to bag up everything, she told her father who hovered nearby, "This was definitely a murder."

While he didn't have any experience in investigating

murders, by his own admission, he nodded in agreement with her assessment. "I'm so glad you're handling this. I'm so happy you got home in time to deal with this, Beth."

She could hear the relief in his voice. But she didn't understand it. Army colonel Mike Snow had always been so capable, so proud and stubborn. What had happened to her father?

Had age mellowed him? Or made him doubt himself?

As she studied him, his face flushed, and he shook his head. "Of course, your mother is going to be furious with me for involving you," he admitted. "She wanted you to relax. She wanted to spend some time with you."

"I will spend plenty of time with Mom," she assured him. "It's going to take the lab a while to get back to us with the autopsy report. We need to know how long the body has been buried and if there's any DNA to identify who she was."

"She?"

She nodded. "I'm pretty sure the skeleton is female." Bethany had started her career with the FBI as a forensics specialist before becoming an agent. It had been her "in" into an agency that was so selective it was tough to even get an interview, which had been so much of its appeal for her. She'd wanted to solve the big cases, the ones nobody else had been able to crack.

Her father sighed. "That's a shame. I can't imagine whose body it might be. Only missing persons reports since I became sheriff of Bear Creek have been for old Mrs. Henshaw when she gets lost on her walks. And I always find her."

"I don't think this person was that old," Bethany

said. "We'll know more when the autopsy report comes back."

"Will it be able to tell us who she is?"

"Depends," she said. "We can get DNA from the bones, but there would have to be some on file to match it to…"

"So if there is no DNA on file for her, she'll just be a Jane Doe?" Her father sounded horrified.

"There are a lot of Jane Does out there," Bethany said. Her job for the past several years had been to discover who they were, and who their killers were, so they could get justice. But for some reason now it didn't seem as important to her as it once had; maybe because she knew there would always be more. She hadn't expected for one to show up here, though.

"That's sad," a deep voice murmured.

Bethany tensed before turning toward Cody. He'd slipped out of his truck and walked up without her noticing. Maybe it was good she was taking a break if she'd been that unaware of her surroundings, of a potential threat. Especially with all those other warnings she'd received.

Cody didn't pose a physical threat, but he unsettled her all the same. He threatened her peace of mind and her heart, just as he had all those years ago.

But she wasn't the giddy teenage girl in love with the most popular boy in school anymore. She was a grown woman with a career she'd always wanted. A career that meant everything to her. But maybe that was because it was all she had.

She focused on that career now, on doing her job.

"Got any thoughts on who your excavator might have dug up?" she asked him.

He shook his head. "I have no idea, Bethany. I've been gone a long time, too. I just returned a few months ago."

She wanted to ask him why he'd come home when he'd been just as determined to stay away as she'd been. No. She wanted to ask him if he'd ever missed her at all, or if he'd fallen harder for Molly's mother than he'd had her. She wanted to ask him all those things but not in front of her father, who was silently studying both their faces.

Cody had no such qualms about asking her questions. "Are you just home for Christmas?"

"Yes." She wasn't even sure she was staying until then, but she wasn't about to admit that in front of her father either.

"Beth is up for a big promotion to run her own unit in the FBI field office in New York City," her father added.

"Congratulations," Cody said. "That's quite impressive. But then you always were."

That praise, coming from him, had her stomach doing a little flip, had her pulse quickening. He had always praised her intelligence and her ambition. He hadn't asked her to give up her dreams, but he'd made her want to. And that had been even more troubling to her than if he'd asked her to...

"What about you?" she asked, gesturing at the equipment. "Why'd you have the excavator out here?"

"Bruce was digging footings for the barn I intend to build to expand the ranch operations to breeding and boarding horses," he explained.

"So you're staying in Bear Creek?" she asked.

He nodded. "That's the plan."

"It's great to have you home," her father told the former rodeo rider. "I'm sure your dad is very happy that you're back, too."

Cody shrugged. "Depends on the day..."

Cody hadn't always had the easiest relationship with his father, at least not when he'd been a teenager and so intent on leaving the ranch. His father had seen his son wanting to leave as a betrayal, like when his wife had left them. The few times Bethany had actually visited with the man over those four years, he'd seemed just as disapproving of her as he had Cody. Maybe he'd blamed her for Cody wanting to leave Bear Creek.

"What about Roberta?" Bethany asked about his stepmother, who was also the town veterinarian. Bethany had always been so impressed that the woman hadn't been like her contemporaries—like Bethany's mother. She'd focused on her education and her career and had made her practice a success long before she'd started dating Cody's dad. Bethany had worked part-time at Roberta's office and had asked her advice about science courses and colleges. "How has she been?"

Cody shrugged again. "I don't know. I've only seen her a couple of times since I came back."

"She doesn't live on the ranch anymore?" Bethany asked with surprise. She'd married Cody's dad and moved into the house shortly before Bethany's family had moved to Bear Creek. And she'd seemed happy remodeling the place to make it a home.

He shook his head. "She divorced my dad a few years ago."

Maybe Roberta had discovered that it wasn't possible to have it all—the practice and the personal life. That was what had kept Bethany from getting serious with anyone. Or at least that was the excuse she gave herself for having dated so infrequently over the past twelve years.

She wasn't so certain that it was the truth. She was worried that Cody might have been the real reason she'd never settled because she had never once felt about anyone she'd dated the way that she had felt about him. So infatuated…

"I'm sorry," Bethany said. She was also sorry that, on their frequent phone calls, she'd stopped her mom whenever Sally Snow had started talking about someone close to Cody, or she might have heard about Roberta leaving his father. Bethany's refusal to listen to anything about Cody was probably the reason her mother hadn't mentioned his move home with his daughter. So she really had only herself to blame for this surprise. It was nothing compared to the shock he must have felt when his excavator had uncovered the skeleton, though.

He shook his head. "No need to apologize to me…" he mumbled. "About that anyways…"

Was there something else he felt she owed him an apology for? Surely he couldn't be angry with her for breaking up with him, not when he'd married and had a child as well as winning all those championships like he'd dreamed of doing.

Her father, who'd barely acknowledged Cody when they'd been dating, reached out now to grab his shoulder. "You didn't need to deal with this body turning up here, not with everything else you have to handle on your own," he said in commiseration.

Cody shook his head. "I've got Sammy to help out. And all the women from the church keep offering to help, too. Molly loves going to preschool there, and she especially loves your wife."

"Every kid does," her father said, and there was the pride in his voice he'd had when he'd talked about Bethany's promotion.

Every kid *had* always loved her mother. All her friends had wanted to hang out at Bethany's house, where her mother made them cookies and listened to their problems. Bethany had preferred to hang out here, at this old homestead on the ranch, with Cody or with Roberta at the veterinary practice.

The rumble of a cell phone vibrating emanated from Bethany's dad's jacket. He reached inside and pulled it out. His lips curved into a wide smile. "Speaking of the love of my life and everyone else's. I better let her know what I've recruited you to do, Beth." With the phone clasped against his ear, he walked to his SUV, jumped inside and closed the door.

And for the first time since her return to Bear Creek, Bethany was alone with Cody in the very same place where she'd left him twelve years ago. That night she'd rushed away from him, worried that if she didn't, she would change her mind. That she'd tell him it was all a mistake and she loved him so much that she couldn't leave him for college, that she would follow him anywhere. But instead, she'd jumped into her car and driven off, and she was surprised that she'd managed to get to town without crashing, with the way tears had filled her eyes.

She drew in a deep breath of crisp winter air and cleared her head enough to focus on what she had to do. On the questions she needed answered. She'd never not solved a case. That was the reason she'd been offered the new position—she was so good at her job. But she could only ask Cody questions about the case; she couldn't ask him the other questions she wanted to ask, like *Did you ever think about me over the years?* Or *Did you ever want to talk to me after that night? To see me?*

Or *Did you forget all about me?*

Before she could ask him anything, he murmured, "It's surreal being here again."

She thought immediately that he was talking about being here, in their place… But jumping to that conclusion would make her look like she hadn't forgotten about them, that she hadn't moved on. So she remarked, "I didn't think you were ever coming back to the ranch— to Bear Creek—once you left."

Beneath the brim of his brown Stetson, he arched his dark blond brows. "I thought the same thing about you."

"I'm only here for the holidays," she said. Even if she turned down that new position, which she'd be a fool to do, there was nothing for her to do in Bear Creek once this cold case was solved. "I'm not staying. You're staying."

He nodded. "I have to…"

"Why?" she asked. "For your daughter? For your dad? What's going on with him?"

"Early onset Alzheimer's," Cody said.

And a pang of sympathy struck her heart so fiercely that she reached out and clasped his arm. Even beneath the denim and the sheepskin lining of his coat, she could feel his muscles tighten, and she pulled her hand away. "I'm sorry, Cody. I didn't know…"

He expelled a ragged breath. "I didn't either…until a few months ago," he said, his voice gruff with self-recrimination.

"That's when you came home?" she asked.

He nodded again. "Yeah. I probably would have anyway," he said. "Things have changed for me since Molly was born. I've changed. I now appreciate growing up here, in Bear Creek, and I think it'll be a good, safe place for her to grow up, too." Then the doors slammed shut on the coroner's van, and the body bag that had just been stowed inside it, and he shuddered as he glanced at it. "Maybe I was wrong…"

"You really have no idea who that could be?" she asked.

He shook his head. "Like you, I've been gone a long time. And I didn't come home as often as I should have. And with Dad's memory being what it is, I'm not sure he would have realized if someone was missing, or if he would have even noticed if someone had been burying something out here…"

"What about your wife?" she asked.

He gasped and jerked back. "What? What about my *ex-wife*?"

"Oh, she's not dead?"

His brow furrowed now when he stared down at her.

"What did you think? That I murdered her and buried her on the ranch? I didn't change that much."

"You got married," she said. "You have a child."

"Yes," he said. "And I would do anything for Molly."

"Getting her mom out of the picture would have ensured that you got full custody," she remarked. "Except for that serial killer case, most of the cold cases I've solved over the years have ended in the arrest of the spouse of the victim." And because of that, she couldn't overlook Cody as a suspect even though she'd once known him so well. The family and friends of the serial killer she'd recently caught had had no idea what he'd been doing, what the mild-mannered middle school teacher had been capable of. His family, coworkers and neighbors had all been so shocked. Except for maybe one person...

Cody's jaw tightened, and he shook his head. "You've changed, too, Bethany. You're so cynical now."

"I got out of Bear Creek," she said. "I found out what the real world is like." Ugly and cruel and disheartening.

He expelled a ragged sigh. "Bear Creek is the real world," he said. "It's the same as any other place where women leave their children. That's what happened with Molly's mother." And with his own but he'd rarely talked about her even during those four years he and Bethany had been so close. "She decided she didn't want to be a wife or mother. She signed over full custody to me."

"I'll need to speak to her, to confirm that."

"That she signed off custody of Molly or that she's still alive?" he asked.

"Cody..."

"Her name is Theresa Muldoon," he said. "I don't have her new cell number, but she's a barrel racer with the rodeo. You could check with my uncle Shep and track her down."

His uncle, his dad's younger brother, was the reason Cody had been so obsessed with the rodeo. Shep Shepard had been a champion rider before an injury sidelined him and he'd become an announcer. "You were going to be like him," she said. "You were going to travel the rodeo circuit forever."

"I grew up," he said. "I'm not the naive eighteen-year-old kid whose heart you broke all those years ago."

His heart hadn't been the only one she'd broken that day; she'd broken her own, too. But she couldn't tell him that, and even if she did, it wouldn't change anything. They had no more chance of a future together now than they'd had all those years ago. They still wanted different things out of life. He was going to stay in Bear Creek to raise his daughter, and she was as anxious as ever to leave again.

She didn't know what to say to him now, and a heavy silence fell between them as snow began to fall from the sky.

"If you have any other questions for me," he said, "you know where to find me. I'm not going anywhere. But right now, I need to get back to my dad and my daughter." He turned then and walked back to his truck.

As he drove off, Bethany acknowledged how right he'd been when he'd said this was surreal. Standing here, in their spot, with fat snowflakes drifting down on the heavy equipment and the mound of dirt and the sheriff SUV and the crime scene vehicles, she felt like she was trapped in some strange snow globe. Like some big hand was shaking it and her, and upending her entire world...

Chapter Four

Cody was so hot with anger that the snow falling on his head and shoulders as he stalked toward the house probably sizzled as it touched him. He stomped his boots across the boards of the back porch and jerked open the door to the kitchen.

"I told you it was a bad idea to date the sheriff's daughter," Don Shepard said the minute Cody stepped inside the house. Don sat at the kitchen table, his gray hair mussed but clean, his brown eyes bleary with confusion. "I knew he'd come gunning for ya, son."

Sammy, who stood at the stove, glanced over his shoulder at Cody and explained, "He heard the sirens and saw the lights. He was worried about what was going on. I told him the sheriff had stopped by to talk to you."

"About his daughter…" Don began.

"I'm not dating the sheriff's daughter." Not anymore and not ever again. He couldn't believe she'd thought he could have killed his wife and buried her on the property. That she could have suspected him of doing something so heinous, so horrendous…

Had she ever really known him at all?

"Then what was he doing here?" his father persisted.

Cody should have been pleased that his dad was lucid enough to remember the lights and sirens, but this was the one time his father's memory loss wouldn't have bothered him. Because he didn't want to tell his dad about the body and upset him even more, he shrugged. "I think Sheriff Snow had some business with one of the hands."

"Probably Tom Campbell," Don said, his voice gruff with disgust. "I had a feeling that guy was no good…"

Sammy's long body stiffened, and he turned away from the stove to ask, "Who's Tom Campbell?"

"A hand who worked the ranch when I was a kid," Cody answered Sammy. Then he reminded his dad, "Tom Campbell doesn't work here anymore."

Campbell had quit around the same time that Cody's mother had taken off. Even as a kid, he probably would have put two and two together, but all the gossip in town had definitely made it clear to him that they had left Bear Creek together. He remembered the guy hanging around, flirting with Kim Shepard. She'd laughed and smiled back at him, probably enjoying his attention since Dad had always been so busy with the ranch. That was probably why she'd chosen to spend the rest of her life with him rather than her son and her husband.

Just as Bethany had chosen college and a career over a life with him. He hadn't asked her to make a choice, to give up on her dreams. He hadn't even had a chance to propose, to promise that they could make it work, that they could stay together.

She hadn't wanted that, hadn't wanted him. Now she

had her degree and her career and tons of accolades proving how good she was at her job. But what else did she have? He hadn't been able to tell if she wore a ring, but surely, if she was married or even seriously involved, that person would have come home with her for the holidays.

Despite all her success and his irritation with her, Cody felt a flash of pity for her. He couldn't imagine not having Molly in his life. He glanced around the kitchen. "Where's the princess?" he asked.

Sammy sighed. "She's probably still staring out the front window, watching to see if Snow White comes back to the house."

He really hoped Bethany didn't come back to the house and ask any more of her terrible questions in front of his daughter. He didn't want to have to get into why Theresa had given up both of them, just like his mom had his dad and him. While Theresa claimed she just hadn't wanted to be a mother or a wife, Cody suspected that his ex-wife had found someone else, someone she'd really loved, just like his mother must have had to have stayed away all these years.

Cody wasn't angry with Theresa, though, and he certainly wouldn't have hurt her. He couldn't even blame her for not loving him; he'd never really loved her the way he should have, the way he'd once loved Bethany Snow. But he would never be able to understand how she'd given up Molly, too.

He needed to see his daughter now, to make certain she was okay, so he hurried out of the kitchen, through the dining room and foyer into the living room. He didn't see her at first, and alarm squeezed his heart. Then he noticed the Molly-size shape behind the heavy curtains, and he pulled them aside to find her with her nose nearly pressed across the glass of the picture window.

"What are you doing, sweetheart?" he asked.

She glanced back at him over her shoulder. "Watching for the lights…"

She wouldn't see them now. With the crime scene between the farmhouse and town, all those vehicles would not pass this way, and for that, Cody was grateful. He didn't want to have to think about what he'd found and to whom that body might belong. It couldn't belong to anyone he knew—not with all the years he'd been away from Bear Creek. The person must have been murdered elsewhere and buried there, maybe by someone just passing through. But the thought of a killer being this close to his home, to his family…

Cody reached out and picked up his daughter, clutching her close against his heart. She was so precious to him; he would do anything to protect her from harm and from any more heartbreak.

"We will put up our own lights this week," Cody promised her. Since he wasn't sure when excavation would resume for the barn, he had time now to get the house and himself ready for the holidays.

Molly had been anxious for them to get a Christmas tree and decorate it, but now she just stared at him with her little brow furrowed beneath wisps of strawberry blond hair. "Isn't Miss Snow and her daddy coming back to the house?"

"No, honey, they're not," he told her.

"Why not?" she asked.

He forced a smile for her when he felt like doing anything but. "They're really busy."

In the four years he'd known Bethany, that had been her biggest complaint about her father. That he was always busy, that even after no longer working for the army, he was never home. It was a bond they'd shared because his dad had always been busy with the ranch, with trying to keep it running to support them and for Cody to take over someday. Cody had helped him work it before and after school, but he hadn't wanted the ranch. He'd wanted to be like Uncle Shep and travel with the rodeo, to become rich and famous. He nearly snorted at his naivete. He knew now how fleeting fame was, and that family was everything.

And Bethany, who'd complained all those years about how her father was always too busy working, now appeared too busy for family, too, or at least to have one of her own. Even though she'd come home for the holidays, Cody doubted she would have any time to enjoy them. Because for the first time that he knew of in Bear Creek history, there had been a murder.

Hopefully she wouldn't come back to question him any more about it, that she was satisfied that he hadn't murdered anyone and buried them on the ranch. The only thing he wished he could have buried here was his memories of her and all the feelings he'd had for her. Tonight, with her treating him like a suspect, he realized how little she'd known him and how little she thought of him. She'd never really loved him like he'd loved her. So maybe now he would finally be able to bury those memories and old feelings even deeper than that skeleton had been buried, so deep that they would never surface again.

Good thing Bethany had brought along her laptop to Bear Creek. She'd had no idea that she would need it for a case, but it had felt too strange for her to be without it or to leave it behind in her apartment. On the way from the crime scene to town, she clicked away on the keyboard, using her cell hot spot for an internet connection. In an FBI database, she found that new cell number Cody didn't have. Why would his ex-wife have wanted no contact with him, with their daughter?

Knowing the usual reason, she checked for any personal protection orders against him or any reports of domestic abuse. The only report that came up with his name had him as a witness to a traffic accident, one where he'd administered first aid at the scene and had been lauded for potentially saving a life. That sounded like the Cody she'd known, the one everyone had admired…the one she'd loved.

But sometimes people presented one side in public and another in private. Like that school-teaching serial killer…

While Cody had always acted the same with her, his wife could have another perspective, another reason for divorcing him. Maybe Bethany wanted to find that reason to justify her breaking up with him all those years ago, to convince herself that she'd done the right thing.

She called that number she'd found for Theresa Muldoon, and when it went directly to voice mail, she said,

"Ms. Muldoon, this is Agent Snow with the Federal Bureau of Investigations. I would appreciate a call back at this number…" and she gave out her cell.

"Who's Ms. Muldoon?" her father asked when she put away her cell and her laptop in her backpack.

"Cody's ex-wife," she said.

Her dad glanced from the road to her and asked, "Why would you want to talk to her? I don't think she's ever even been to Bear Creek. She wouldn't know anything about that body Cody found."

"I want to make sure that body's not hers," Bethany admitted.

Her father shook his head. "Of course it's not. How could you even consider that as a possibility?"

"My job is to consider all possibilities and rule out the ones I can," she said. She wouldn't have solved as many cases as she had if she hadn't been suspicious of everyone involved. But that suspicion, that cynicism, had taken a toll on her, and sometimes she missed the naive girl she'd once been. "That's why I want to touch base with her."

"I don't know much about murder investigations," her father said, "but I can tell when something's been buried a long time. That body's been there a long time, Beth. It can't be Molly's mother."

Heat rushed to her face as she realized he was probably right. But she shrugged. "Like I said, I'm just ruling out all possibilities."

"Okay." He didn't sound convinced.

Probably because Bethany wasn't convinced, herself, that it was her only motive. She wasn't sure what her motivation was for leaving that voice mail, for wanting to talk to Cody's ex.

"Is that why Cody left like he did? When I was on the phone with your mother?" he asked. "Did you treat him like a suspect?"

"He is a suspect," she said.

And her father gasped now. "How? Why?"

"The body was found on his property."

"Because he had it dug up," her father interjected. "He wouldn't have chosen that spot to excavate if he'd known what was there. Whoever buried that body way out there didn't want it to ever be found."

She sighed. Her father was right that it didn't make sense for Cody to uncover what he'd buried, but she couldn't take any chances. She couldn't let her personal feelings make her rule anyone out or in too soon in an investigation. "I just need to be sure…"

"About that body or about Cody?" he asked.

She needed to do her job, but she also wouldn't mind getting closure on her decision to end their relationship after graduation. She wasn't about to admit that to her father. "The first thing I need to do is find out who the victim is," she said. "Then we can notify her family, bring them some closure."

"Like you did for the victims of that serial killer," her father said. "You gave those families some peace."

She wasn't sure she had. Some of them had blamed her for their private pain going public, like she'd sought out attention for solving those cases, like she'd exploited their personal tragedies for her career gain. Maybe that was why she hadn't accepted that position yet; she didn't want to profit off the loss of others. Then there were those threats…

"I'm not so sure about that…" she admitted.

Her father steered his SUV into the driveway of the two-story brick colonial house in town where Bethany had spent the last four years of her childhood. He shut off the ignition and glanced over at her. "Are you okay, Beth?" he asked. "Your mother's been worried about you."

"Mom worries too much," she said.

He chuckled and nodded. "Yes, she does. But that's just because she loves you so much and wants you to be happy."

Happy.

The word startled Bethany because it wasn't one she'd given much thought to. Success. The satisfaction of closing cases and getting justice. That was what she'd been focused on these past twelve years. Climbing the career ladder and making a difference in the world, getting killers off the street. But her own happiness…

Her father pushed open the door and stepped out. "We better get inside. She's been holding dinner for us. And she isn't happy that I involved you in this case."

Bethany met her dad at the back door, which he held open so she could step inside first. She hadn't been back here in so long, but it smelled the same as always, the same as every place they'd ever lived—like a home-cooked meal and cookies baking. Warmth flooded her the minute she walked into the big, open kitchen, and it didn't have as much to do with the heat from the double ovens as with her mother pulling her into a tight embrace.

"Oh, my baby…" Sally Snow whispered. "I'm so happy you're home."

Tears stung Bethany's eyes. Nobody hugged like her mother, with such love and exuberance. "Mom…" Emotions rushed over her. For the second time that night she felt like a teenager again. Except that when she'd been a teenager, her mother's hugs had embarrassed her, and she'd wriggled away at the first opportunity. Except for once…

Tonight—like that night—she appreciated it, and instead of pulling back, she closed her free arm around her mom and held on for a moment, inhaling the food smells from her auburn hair. For once, her mother was the one who pulled back first, but just to cup Bethany's face in her warm hands and study her. "Are you all right, sweetheart?"

A smile tugged at Bethany's lips. Her hugging back must have surprised and concerned her mother, who studied her with a worried expression on her face. Bethany studied her back. There were new wrinkles on her mother's face, by her mouth and eyes. Laugh lines. And her hair wasn't entirely auburn anymore; there was a thick streak of white coming out of her widow's peak. Despite all the baking and cooking she did, her mother was as fit as she ever was, but then she was always moving, always doing something, always taking care of somebody.

"I'm fine," Bethany assured her. "How are you?"

"Irritated with your father," she said. "I can't believe he brought you out to a crime scene before even bringing you home from the airport."

Repentant, her father leaned down and kissed her

mother's cheek. "Sally, I'm sorry. But this kind of crime scene isn't something I can handle without help."

"So get the state police to take over," she suggested. "Bethany came home to relax and enjoy Christmas with us. Not to investigate a murder." Her hands were still on Bethany's face as she continued to study her so intently that Bethany felt vulnerable, as if her mother could see something that Bethany didn't even know was there. Like the truth…or maybe the dark circles beneath her eyes revealed how exhausted she was—physically, mentally, emotionally.

"She needs a break, Mike," her mom continued. "Respite from the horrors of her job."

Had her mother somehow figured out the toll that career-making case had taken on Bethany? Probably. Sally had always been able to tell when Diana or one of their friends had gotten her feelings hurt or her heart broken. And that night, when Bethany had come home from her and Cody's special place, her mother had been waiting for her as if she'd known exactly what she was going to do, that she'd intended to break up with the love of her young life. Her mom hadn't asked her anything that night; she'd just offered one of those hugs, and that had probably been the first time Bethany had hugged her back without pulling away first.

In the weeks after their breakup, Bethany had tried to forget their silly teenage fantasy of making a long-distance relationship work. Of their plans for Cody to visit her at school and for her to spend her summers traveling around the rodeo circuit with him. She'd known that would have been too hard—on both of them. That she would have missed him too much when he was gone, and that every knock at her door, she would have hoped was his. And she would have eventually had to disappoint him during the summer when she had to work internships instead of traveling with him.

She'd ended it before they could disappoint and miss each other, and had tried so hard to forget about him. Had he thought about her after? He'd gotten married and started a family when he'd once sworn so convincingly that she was the only woman he would ever consider marrying.

She should focus on the present, like Cody was.

To assuage her mother's worries and her irritation with her dad, Bethany smiled before stepping back so that her mom's hands fell away from her face. "I'm fine, Mom." She dropped her backpack onto the hardwood floor and settled onto one of the stools at the big kitchen island. Every day after school, this island had had kids lined up at it, her friends, her siblings' friends and some of the neighbors.

"You should have seen her working the scene, Sal," her dad said as he slid his arm around his wife's shoulders. "She'll get this case closed faster than any state trooper could."

Bethany hoped that was true for a couple of reasons. She didn't want to disappoint her father, who was showing the pride in her and the attention she'd always sought from him. And for another, she didn't want to see any more of Cody Shepard than she had to.

She hadn't intended to see him at all this trip.

"How was it?" her mom asked.

"The crime scene?" Bethany asked. Her mother had

never shown any interest in her cases before, just in her health and her happiness.

"Seeing Cody Shepard again," her mother said. "How was that? And did you get to meet his adorable little girl?"

Bethany's father chuckled. "You certainly have a fan in her, Sally. She was quite taken with Agent Snow here, too."

"She's a special kid," her mother said with a smile full of warmth and deep affection for the child. "Cody's done an amazing job with her."

He'd told Bethany that he'd changed, that he'd grown up. He wasn't the boy she'd known, the one desperate to leave Bear Creek and never come back. That boy had wanted no responsibilities in his life, only the rodeo and her. Now he had more responsibilities than she had—with the ranch, with his daughter and with his dad.

"Cody's quite the man," her mother continued, and she was obviously fishing for a reaction from Bethany.

Her dad chuckled again. "Don't go thinking they're going to reunite, Sally. Not after your daughter interrogated him like a murder suspect."

Her mother gasped. "You did what? Bethany, how could you?"

"Because I'm doing my job," she reminded her mom. "And a body was found on his ranch. So of course I have to question him."

"But like a suspect?" her father chimed in.

Bethany sighed and closed her eyes as a wave of exhaustion struck her. She hadn't been sleeping well, or really much at all, since working the serial killer case. So many young women had lost their lives because of that madman. And he'd been someone's husband, someone's father, son, brother and apparently an idol to someone else. She swallowed down a wave of revulsion over that and focused on her family instead. "You were in your truck talking to Mom, so you don't know how I spoke to him," she reminded her father.

He narrowed his blue eyes and stared at her. "I know that he jumped in his truck and drove off."

"He had to get back to his daughter and his dad," she said, which was the truth. Just not the complete truth…

"Poor Cody," her mother said, and she made a tsking noise with her tongue. "So much on his shoulders."

"He has Sammy," Bethany said, smiling slightly with amusement that when Cody had said the name, she'd thought he'd been talking about his wife.

Her father's long body tensed, and the smile slid away from his face. He'd been standing behind her on the porch earlier this afternoon, so she hadn't seen his reaction then to little Molly's nanny.

"What?" she asked her dad. "Don't you approve of a male nanny—a manny?"

He shook his head. "It's not that…just the vibe I get from the man. He didn't seem real thrilled to see us at the ranch, especially you, Agent Snow."

She furrowed her brow as she studied her father's face. "What? Do you think there's an outstanding warrant on him?"

"Lot of people join things like the rodeo or carnivals so they keep moving, so they're never in one place long enough to get caught," her father said.

"Sounds like you could have handled this case without any help at all," she said.

He shook his head. "Oh, no…"

She narrowed her eyes and studied her dad again. His skin was so pale, and despite her mother's infamous baking and cooking, he looked thinner than the last time she'd seen him. She wanted to ask him if there was anything wrong, but before she had the chance, her cell vibrated within the backpack at her feet. And she reached down and grabbed it.

Was it Cody's ex-wife? Was she returning her call already?

But when she pulled the cell from her bag, her landlord's contact flashed on the screen. "Hello, Mr. Reynolds," she greeted him. "Is everything all right?"

He never called unless there was some issue going on with the half of the duplex she rented from him. He lived in the other half. "Bethany, I just noticed that your place was broken into. A window on your back bedroom is broken, and it wasn't like that earlier today."

"No, it wasn't," she said. That back bedroom was where she had her home office, where her laptop had been before she'd packed it up.

"I called the police. They should be here soon."

"Please, wait for them," she advised. "The intruder might still be there…" And she didn't want her landlord getting hurt. Even though he was a veteran, like her father, he was older and not fit enough to fight off an attacker.

The older man snorted. "I'm fine. I used my key to come inside. Your TV is here. But it looks like somebody went through your stuff…maybe looking for cash or jewelry…"

She chuckled. "They wouldn't find anything like that

in my place," she said. But she wondered if that was really what they'd been looking for or if the break-in had been about the serial killer case and all the media attention over it. Some kooks had come out of the woodwork as fans of the killer, and they resented that she'd caught him.

That she'd stopped him. She'd received some threats that they were going to stop her next. That she would be the serial killer's final victim. So had they been looking for something to steal or for her?

To kill her...

Chapter Five

When Cody drove past the old homestead on his way to church Sunday morning, he was glad the site was far enough off the road that Molly couldn't see the yellow crime scene tape from her passenger window. She'd already had so many questions the past couple of days about Bethany and the Snow family. Fortunately Bethany must not have had any more questions for him since she hadn't come back to the house.

That had disappointed Molly, who had a strange fascination with her even though she'd only met her the once and just spoken for minutes. Was it because Bethany was so beautiful? Or because she was Mrs. Snow's daughter? Cody didn't know why his daughter was so captivated by her. But he wished she wasn't. And he really wished he wasn't still captivated as well.

She wasn't the Bethany he remembered. Just as he'd told her that he'd grown up and changed, clearly so had she. She was so cynical now. So suspicious.

He might have been, too, after his mother leaving him, after his wife leaving him, but he had Molly. And

her pure and loving heart reminded him of all the good-
ness in the world yet, making it impossible for him to
be cynical. He loved his little girl so much he wanted
to make her as happy as she made him. "We'll get the
Christmas tree after church and decorate it," he told
her. He would have done it a couple of days ago, but
he hadn't wanted to go to town to buy the decorations.
Having grown up in Bear Creek, he knew all too well
that there would be only one thing everybody was talking about in town: the body.

He hadn't wanted to think about it himself let alone
have Molly overhear anything. Even now, he wasn't sure
how he would shut down any intrusive questions. But
he was going to do his best to protect Molly from the
gory details.

At least in church, he wouldn't have to worry; the
community in the small-town church was very tight-knit
and protective, especially of his daughter. His father had
never been much of a churchgoer, but some of Cody's
best memories of his mother, from those first ten years
of his life, were of her bringing him to church and then
to Sunday school afterward. He'd wanted those same
memories, that faith and those values for his daughter,
and so he'd started attending when they'd moved back
a few months ago and had enrolled her in the church
preschool program.

In her booster chair in the passenger's seat, she was
smiling wide and singing Sunday school songs. "Jesus
loves me…"

"Yes, he does," Cody murmured. "And so does Daddy."

She turned toward him and offered him that big, bright
smile. "I love you, too, Daddy."

Warmth flooded his heart, expanding it so that he loved her even more than he had just minutes before. "You are the most special little girl in the whole world," he told her.

She giggled. "Do you know all the little girls in the whole world?" she challenged him.

How was she so smart?

"Well, no…"

"Then you don't know that I'm the most special," she pointed out.

"You are the most special girl in *my* whole world," he told her.

She smiled and nodded. "Okay, Daddy, but your world isn't very big."

"It's you…" he said. She was his whole world.

"And Sammy and Grandpa and the ranch and church," she added, pretty much summing it up as he turned the truck into the parking lot.

He smiled and leaned across the console to kiss her nose where there was the faintest smattering of freckles.

She laughed.

"Okay," he said. "Let's get all the giggles and the wiggles out before we go in."

This was something his mother had always done with him because he'd been such a hyperactive kid that it had been hard for him to keep quiet and still for very long. She had sympathized because she'd been a wild child in her youth. Townspeople had told him over the years that they'd been more surprised when she'd married his father than when she'd left him. But in those first ten years of his life, Cody remembered her being happy. And making him happy.

As they did every day when Cody dropped Molly at preschool and every Sunday before going inside for the service, they waved their arms and legs around and laughed uproariously. To anyone outside the truck, they probably looked ridiculous. But Cody had never cared, until now when he glanced out the passenger's window on the other side of his laughing daughter and saw Bethany Snow staring in at them, her blue eyes wide with surprise.

He froze, and Molly turned to look at what he was looking at and exclaimed, "Snow White!" She unlocked and pushed open her door.

Cody rushed around to her side to help her down. But she had already unbuckled her booster seat and was wriggling out of it, her feet dangling above the running board. Bethany must have been worried that she was going to slip or fall because she'd stepped forward and had grasped his daughter's waist. "Careful," she said as she helped her down onto the pavement. Once she had, she released her and stepped back.

Molly whirled around and looped her arms around Bethany's waist, hugging her. "Thank you, Snow White."

Bethany's father, who stood on the driver's side of his wife's minivan, chuckled. "She keeps thinking you're a princess."

"*She's* the princess," Bethany's mother said as she came around the back of her vehicle and joined them.

"Mrs. Snow!" Molly exclaimed. She released Bethany, rushed to the older woman and grabbed her for a tight hug.

"You'd think it had been weeks since they saw each

other," Cody remarked, aiming his comment more at Bethany's father than her, "but it was just Friday morning." And that afternoon they'd checked in at the excavation site where that body had been unearthed.

"I didn't know Mom was teaching preschool…" Bethany stared at her mother and his daughter, her brow slightly furrowed.

"She's been teaching it since you left for college," her father said. "Needed something to keep her busy with all you kids out of the house." His brow furrowed now. "And with me not being home like I should have been…"

A gasp of shock slipped out of Bethany's lips at her father's admission. Before she could say anything, the church bells began to chime.

Molly wriggled down from Mrs. Snow's arms and grabbed her hand, tugging her toward the church. "We better get inside. Can me and Daddy sit with you and Sheriff Snow and Snow White?"

"Of course," Mrs. Snow replied with a chuckle. "I'd love that." The two of them rushed off toward the open doors with the sheriff following close behind, leaving Cody standing alone in the parking lot with Bethany.

His reluctance to join them must have shown on his face because Bethany assured him, "Don't worry. I won't interrogate you in church."

"Maybe you should," Cody suggested. "Would make it hard for me to lie."

"Have you lied to me?" she asked.

"Never." He wondered if she could say the same, or had she lied to him that night so many years ago when she'd told him she'd never really loved him? How could he have loved her so much if she'd never returned those feelings? "What about you?" he asked.

She started again, like she had over her father's admission, and her face flushed with embarrassment. Or was it the cold? While it wasn't freezing, the breeze was chilly and carried a few fat snowflakes on it like it had that couple of nights ago when they'd stood in their old spot.

Due to the cold, most of the rest of the congregation had rushed toward the open doors and the warmth of the church. But instead of rushing past them, one woman stopped and joined them, so Bethany didn't answer him. He wondered if she would have had they not been interrupted.

"This feels like old times," Dr. Roberta Kline remarked, "stumbling upon you two staring at each other…"

"Dr. Kline," Bethany said and reached out to hug the woman she'd once idolized. "It's wonderful to see you."

"Roberta," the woman said as she clasped Bethany back. "How many times have I told you to call me Roberta?"

"Roberta," Bethany dutifully replied just as she had when she'd been a teenager and his stepmother had insisted she call her by her first name, and that had been many times, since Bethany had worked part-time at her veterinary practice.

The older woman turned toward Cody then, offering him a smile that didn't quite reach her dark eyes. "Hi, Cody. How's your dad doing?"

He shrugged. "You know…good days and bad days…"

"Yes, I know," she said, and the smile slipped away from his former stepmother's lips. "I'm really sorry…"

She'd apologized to him before, and like before, he just nodded in acceptance of it. He'd never been close to her. Bethany had spent more time with her than he had. He'd either been busy with school, helping his dad on the ranch or hanging out with Bethany at their special place.

Roberta drew in a shaky breath and glanced from one to the other again. "I heard that a body was found out on the ranch."

Cody shuddered and nodded. "Yeah, the excavator dug it up."

"We should go inside," Bethany said with a pointed glance toward the usher standing at the open doors, "and find my parents and your daughter."

Heat rushed to his face that he'd let Molly slip away from him without a thought. But his daughter's bond with Mrs. Snow was so strong he never worried that anything would happen to her. Or he hadn't until the other night. Whoever had been in that barrel had once been someone's child. Now he was anxious to be with his again.

"Yes," he agreed, and he reached out to guide Bethany toward the doors, but when his hand touched her back, she stiffened. "Sorry," he murmured. Maybe it had been more the force of old habits than politeness that had compelled him to touch her, because he'd looked for any excuse when they'd been teenagers.

"He's old-fashioned like his father," Roberta remarked. "Thinks a woman needs help opening and walking through doors. Cody, you need to remember that Bethany is a strong, independent woman."

She'd made that clear to him when she'd dumped him. He wasn't able to forget no matter how much he'd tried over the years. "Then I guess it won't be rude if I go inside first," he said, and he rushed ahead of them to find his daughter.

At least she still needed him...

But with the way she was clasping Mrs. Snow's hand, it didn't look as if she intended to let go until Bethany joined them on the bench. Then she reached for her hand instead, and while Bethany stiffened a bit again and her blue eyes widened with surprise, she closed her hand around Molly's little one and held onto it all through the service.

At the end, before Molly headed off to Sunday school with Mrs. Snow, she asked Bethany, "Will you please, please come to our house today and help us decorate the tree?"

He was the one who stiffened then. He couldn't let his daughter get too attached to Bethany. It was only going to lead to the same heartbreak for his daughter that it had for him. Because she wasn't staying in Bear Creek.

"Miss Bethany is really busy, honey," he told his little girl. "She doesn't have time for decorating." She had to find out whose body had been buried on his ranch and then she needed to find out who'd buried it. And once she did, she would leave for that new position her father had mentioned. There was no way Bethany was going to turn down a promotion, not when all that had ever mattered to her was having a career.

Why hadn't she been able to turn down the offer?

Bethany had never had a problem saying no before, especially to all the men who'd asked her for drinks or dinner. But Cody hadn't been the one who'd invited her to his house; his daughter had. And when Bethany had stared down into that sweet face, she hadn't been able to say no to the child.

So she found herself standing on his front porch as she had the other night, waiting for someone to answer the doorbell. This time, Bethany's father was not beside her; she was alone. Like she usually was…

The door opened, and a little dynamo reached out and hugged Bethany's waist. "You're here!" Molly exclaimed. "Daddy, I told you Snow White would come!"

She smiled and shook her head. "I'm not Snow White." She was not that sweet and pure, not after everything she'd seen. The horrible things… "You need to call me Bethany."

"Miss Bethany," Cody corrected her as he appeared in the open doorway. "And you need to get inside, Miss Molly, before you catch a cold for Christmas."

Molly giggled as she tugged Bethany inside with her, and Cody closed the door behind them. Before Bethany could take off her boots and her coat, Molly pulled her through the foyer into the living room where a tall, bare pine tree stood in front of the picture window. "Look," she said. "Look at the tree. It looks so sad now. We have to dress it up and make it pretty…just like you."

Bethany hadn't dressed up specifically for the tree trimming, but she still wore the red sweater and wool slacks that she'd worn to church that morning. And she'd put on some lipstick and mascara for once. Her face flushed that she'd done that—not for herself but for Cody. Maybe because she wanted him to look at her the way he used to look at her…

But after the way she'd treated him that night so long ago, and that night just a couple of days ago, she didn't expect that to actually happen. She didn't expect him to actually forgive her. Not that it mattered to her anymore, not that *he* mattered to her anymore.

Solving the crime that had been discovered on his property was the only thing that mattered. But Molly, with her sweetness and friendliness, was making it hard to focus on only that.

"You're the pretty one," Bethany said. The little girl looked just like her father with that strawberry blond hair and those bright green eyes. From the driver's license photograph of her that Bethany had pulled up, Theresa Muldoon had dark hair and eyes.

Theresa hadn't returned Bethany's call yet, probably because she didn't believe Bethany was actually an FBI agent and not just some phone scammer. Bethany didn't really believe that the woman had been buried on her ex-husband's property. Cody could not have changed that much. But until she had confirmation, she couldn't rule out anything. The coroner from the state police was working on determining time of death, but with only skeletal remains, that was difficult to pinpoint, especially when the remains had been encapsulated in a barrel like they had. The only thing the coroner had confirmed so far was that the skeleton had belonged to a woman and that cause of death had been a blow to the head, just as Bethany had surmised.

She'd come to Bear Creek because she'd wanted a break from murder, from tragedy, but there was apparently no escaping from it—even here. Maybe that was why she hadn't been able to say no to Molly Shepard, because the little girl was so adorable that she reminded Bethany that there was good in the world yet. That morning at church, Bethany had felt more at peace than she had in a long time…even though Cody had been unsettlingly close to her. He affected her just as much as he always had; just the touch of his hand on the small of her back, even with her heavy jacket, had felt like a jolt through her entire body. That was why she'd tensed up like she had, not out of indignation like he or Roberta had thought, but fear.

Fear that he still got to her.

Fear that she might have made a mistake all those years ago. She hadn't let herself consider that before, hadn't really let herself think about him at all lately, but now that she was back in Bear Creek and so was he…

Branches on the tree suddenly rustled, shaking flakes of snow onto Bethany and the hardwood floor. A startled cry slipped through her lips, and she automatically reached for her holster. But it wasn't there. Not wanting a weapon around the child, she'd locked her Glock in the glove box of the sheriff's department SUV her father had insisted she use while she was in Bear Creek. Since a deputy's recent retirement, they had an extra one.

"There's Snowball!" Molly exclaimed as a white kitten dangled from one of the branches.

Cody reached around Bethany and gently plucked the squirming ball of fur from the branch. "Your kitty thinks the Christmas tree is an early present just for her," he told his daughter. Then his face twisted into a grimace. "I think she got some sap on her."

"Sap?" Molly asked, her brow furrowing beneath her wispy bangs.

"It's like syrup," Cody explained. "It comes out of the tree. We need to wash it off her."

"Use some dish soap," Bethany suggested. "My mom always swears that it's the best cleaner."

"I'll get some from Sammy," Molly said and rushed off, leaving her kitten stuck to her father's big hand.

The little thing nipped at Cody's fingers as it tried tugging its fur from his skin. Bethany chuckled and remarked, "Looks like Snowball wants to get away from you."

His shoulders slumped a bit even as he mumbled, "I should be used to that by now..."

She was so curious that she couldn't resist asking, "Are you talking about me or your ex-wife?"

"Both," he replied. "Have you talked to her yet? Have you cleared me of suspicion? Or did you come out here to question me some more?"

Heat rushed to her face. She had wanted to ask him some more questions, not answer his, but she replied, "She hasn't called me back yet."

"Pull up the coverage of yesterday's rodeo in Cheyenne," he said. "You'll see her winning the barrel racing event."

While his shoulders had slumped, hers lifted with the news. It was proof of what she already knew but welcome all the same. But then she felt a twinge of something she couldn't identify, something that might have been jealousy, that Cody still watched his ex-wife compete. Was he still in love with her?

He must have loved her a lot in order to marry and start a family with her. But she ignored that twinge of jealousy and focused on her case while she had the chance to question him. "What about your mother?" Kim Shepard had left long before Bethany and her family had moved to Bear Creek.

"I can't tell you where to find her," he said.

"What if you did?" she asked.

He tensed. "What do you mean? That body…"

She nodded.

He shook his head. "No. My mother packed up all her clothes and stuff and took off years ago, leaving just her wedding ring behind. That's not her."

"Then help me rule her out," she said.

"How?" he asked. "I told you that I don't know where to find her."

She wondered if he'd ever really looked, or if he'd been too hurt by her abandonment to ever seek her out. But what if she hadn't abandoned him? What if someone had taken her away from him?

"Hey, there" came a deep voice, startling her again. Because she'd just been thinking about him. About Don Shepard.

Over the past twelve years, he'd aged even more than her father had. His face was heavily wrinkled, and all of his hair was gray and stood up as if he'd just awoken. And maybe he had. His eyes weren't quite focused yet as he stared at her.

"You're that Snow girl…" he muttered. "I thought you left for college and were never coming back."

"Hello, Mr. Shepard. I'm just home for the holidays."

He nodded. "Your mama will be happy about that. How much school you got left? A couple years?"

While he'd recognized her, he'd clearly forgotten how much time had really passed since he'd seen her last. Seeing the former strong and stoic rancher looking so old and frail and confused brought out a surge of sympathy in Bethany, for him and for Cody.

"Grandpa!" Molly exclaimed as she rushed back into the living room with Sammy close behind her. "Are you going to help us decorate the tree?"

The old man looked down at her, and he looked so confused and almost frightened. "I—I…" He turned toward Cody then, as if he was the only one he recognized. "Where'd your mother go? She was here and now she's gone…"

She'd been gone a lot longer than Bethany had, so clearly Don Shepard had lost all concept of time. He had no idea how many years had passed. Or maybe he did because tears suddenly filled his eyes. "I'm so confused."

"It's okay, Dad," Cody said.

"Are you okay, Grandpa?" Molly asked with concern. She must have seen those tears, too.

"Your grandpa hasn't eaten lunch yet," Sammy said. "So I'll take him into the kitchen for something to eat. I'll make some hot cocoa, too, for you and your daddy and…" His throat moved as if he was choking on her title before he spit out, "Agent Snow." He handed over the bottle of dish soap he was holding. "And here's this for cleaning up Snowball…"

Cody took the bottle in his free hand. "Thanks, Sammy."

The man just nodded before taking Don Shepard's arm and steering him toward the kitchen.

"Molly, why don't you get started on the tree while Miss Bethany helps me with Snowball?" Cody said.

"I wanna help with Snowball, too," she said.

"But you know how Snowball feels about baths," he said.

Molly grimaced. "I'll get all the decorations ready."

"How does Snowball feel about baths?" Bethany asked.

"She doesn't like 'em," Molly said.

Moments later Bethany realized that was an understatement as she and Cody struggled to keep the screaming, clawing kitten in the deep sink in the laundry room as they bathed her. "I thought you just asked me to help so that you could talk to me," she said.

"I did," he admitted. "I wanted to ask how I can help you rule out that that body belongs to my mother."

She nodded. "You can give me something that might have her DNA on it."

"She packed up all her stuff and took it with her when she left," Cody said.

She swallowed down the sudden rush of sympathy she felt for him and forced herself to be professional. "What about the wedding ring you said she left behind?"

He sighed. "My dad kind of lost it when he found she'd left it here but had taken all her other things…and he threw it out."

He would have been so young that that must have been frightening and devastating for him. Sympathy had tears stinging her eyes now, but she blinked them back and focused on Snowball in the sink. "Well…"

"There's nothing," Cody murmured.

Bethany looked at him then. He didn't look anything like his father even before Don Shepard had aged so much. "You..." she said. "I could get a DNA sample from you. It would be a close enough match to hers to identify the body."

"That body isn't hers," Cody insisted.

"Then help me rule it out," she challenged him again.

He nodded. "Fine."

"Daddy! Miss Bethany!" Molly called out. "The hot cocoa is ready!"

Cody rubbed a towel over the kitten's wet fur. "She's excited about tonight," he said. "About decorating the tree. About you..."

"I don't think this is a good idea, Cody," Bethany said. "I'm not staying in Bear Creek."

"I know it's not a good idea," Cody said. "I didn't think you'd say yes when Molly asked. Why did you?"

She wished she knew. "She's hard to say no to," she said.

He sighed. "Yes, she is. But I wonder if that's your real reason or if you wanted to come out again to investigate... to interrogate me and my dad."

"I have a job to do," she reminded him.

He nodded. "So do I. When will you release the crime scene?"

She shrugged. "Soon." The techs had the barrel and the body and hadn't found anything else even after another couple of days of inspecting the scene.

He nodded again. "Good."

Realizing she wasn't welcome in his home, she said, "I guess I should leave now..."

He sighed. "I would like you to stay, to help Molly,"

he said. "She'll be heartbroken if you leave before decorating the tree."

So Bethany found herself drinking cocoa and singing
Christmas carols as they strung lights and hung bulbs.
Instead of feeling self-conscious and silly, like she'd
thought she would, she felt freer, lighter…more at ease
than she had in years. Except for when she looked at
Cody. Then her pulse quickened, and it got just a little
harder to breathe.

He was so good-looking and such a good father. He
was loving and patient with his little girl, lifting her onto
his shoulders so that she could put the star on top of the
tree. Then he clicked the remote that had come with the
lights they'd strung, and the tree lit up with a multitude
of twinkling lights in every color. "All done," he said.

Bethany knew she had to leave before she got any more
used to this, to them…to being part of this family. "I—I
better get home," she said. The afternoon had passed
quickly, too quickly, and night had fallen, wrapping the
old ranch house in darkness. "I didn't realize what time
it was…" Her mother was already upset her father had
enlisted her to help with this case. She should head home
and spend some time with her parents.

"Miss Bethany," Molly began in protest.

But Bethany shook her head. "I don't want to be late
for dinner." Again.

She grabbed the coat she'd tossed onto the couch and
rushed out before even putting it on. She would call
Cody down to the sheriff's office to get that DNA sample. Right now she just needed to get away. She quickly
started the SUV and drove off toward town. Shortly

after she passed the old homestead, lights appeared on the road behind her. As if a vehicle had been at the crime scene...

Why?

Had the driver been returning to the scene of the crime?

Chapter Six

When Bethany left so abruptly, Molly was clearly disappointed. She wasn't the only one, but Cody didn't care about his own feelings. He cared only about his daughter, about making her happy. "Hey, sweetie," he said. "Miss Bethany is in Bear Creek to visit with her mom and dad. That's why she had to leave, to spend time with them."

He wasn't convinced that was the real reason she'd taken off as abruptly as she had. Maybe she was anxious to find footage of that Cheyenne rodeo and confirm if he'd been telling the truth about Theresa. He wasn't sure if she wanted to find him innocent or guilty, though. He just wanted her to find out the truth and close this case. He suspected that wasn't going to be so easy. Not when that body could belong to anyone...

But not his ex-wife or his mom. Those women had left of their own accord.

Because they hadn't cared about their families.

Because they hadn't wanted families, just like Bethany had once told him she didn't. At least she'd told him before they'd gotten married, before they'd had children, but not before he'd fallen so deeply in love with her he'd never quite made it back to the surface. Even tonight, with her singing and laughing with his daughter, he'd felt himself slipping under again.

It was good that she'd left.

"We need to have our dinner, too," he told his daughter. "You stay here and make sure Snowball doesn't climb up in the tree again, and I'll check on Sammy and Grandpa." Maybe it was his imagination but it almost seemed as if Sammy didn't like Bethany or wanted to avoid her for some reason. He'd made himself scarce since she'd arrived at the ranch.

Cody hadn't seen the two men leave the kitchen, but he'd been so preoccupied with Bethany that he might not have noticed. The music had also been playing loudly as they'd sung along to those Christmas carols. He clicked off the radio now, and an almost eerie silence gripped the house.

He nervously broke it, calling out, "Dad? Sammy?" as he headed toward the kitchen. Nobody replied, and when he stepped into the kitchen, he found it empty. Something bubbled inside a pot on the stove, the flame burning low beneath it.

Sammy wouldn't have gone far and left that unattended, not with Dad and Molly and the kitten in the house. He was always so careful, to make sure no one inadvertently hurt themselves. A plate sat on the table, a sandwich on it untouched.

Was that his father's late lunch?

It was nearly dinner time now. How could his dad have gone so long without eating? Dad's stomach should have rumbled and reminded him that he needed to eat. Where was he?

"Dad?" he called out again as he walked around the house, searching every room only to find it empty. He circled back to the kitchen then and opened the back door. Sammy's big black truck was usually parked near it, but it was gone now. The only trace of it were the tracks left in the light snow.

Sammy must have gone somewhere and taken Cody's father with him.

But where and why? And why hadn't he let Cody know that they were leaving?

Was it because of Bethany? Had he not wanted to intrude? Or was there another reason Sammy seemed so reticent with the FBI agent?

Cody reached into his shirt pocket and pulled out his cell. But when he pushed in Sammy's contact, the call went directly to voice mail. Had Sammy shut off his phone?

That wasn't like him. Not at all...

Sammy had been one of the few people in Cody's life that he'd been able to count on. When Cody had shown up on the circuit as a green kid, Sammy had quickly taken him in, had protected and guided him to stay away from the drinkers and rabble-rousers. His father, before his illness, had been the first person Cody had counted on. Don Shepard had worked hard to support him financially even if he hadn't always been emotionally available. Maybe that was because he'd stoically buried his own feelings to protect Cody's...

He'd never said a bad word about Cody's mother, unlike the other people in Bear Creek who told him about the wild child she'd been in high school and how bored she must have been at the ranch. Cody suspected that despite her leaving them, his father had never stopped loving Kim Shepard. He'd married Roberta eventually, when Cody was in his early teens, but Cody had always wondered if Don had done that more for Cody than for himself. He'd thought a child should have a mother. Not that he and Roberta had ever been close. She'd been busy with her veterinarian practice and remodeling the ranch. Still, Cody hadn't given her much of a chance to get close to him; he'd been all right without a mother.

Would Molly? Cody loved her enough for both parents, but could he nurture her enough, support her as much as she deserved, as she needed?

"Daddy?" a soft voice said, drawing his attention back to the kitchen. "Why do you have the door open?"

He shivered as the coldness suddenly penetrated his clothes and his brain. For the first time he understood a little of how his father must feel, unable to focus… easily distracted…

"I was looking for Grandpa and Sammy," he said.

She peered around the kitchen, too. "Where did they go?"

"I don't know…"

And that worried him.

A lot. So much so that his heart was beginning to beat faster and harder with concern. His cell phone still in his hand, he redialed Sammy's number. But just as before, it went directly to voice mail, to the generic recording that came with the phone since Sammy hadn't recorded his own message. "This subscriber is currently unavailable. Please leave a message."

Knowing Sammy never played his messages, Cody ended the call and reached for the keys for his truck. He had to look for them.

Where could they have gone? And were they all right?

Bethany kept glancing at her rearview mirror, checking to see if that vehicle was still behind her. It had to have pulled off the gravel two-track road that led back to the old homestead. What had the driver been doing back there?

Just looking around out of curiosity?

There had certainly been a lot of that at church this morning. Once her mother and Molly had left the community room at the back of the church for Sunday school, it had seemed as if everyone else, even the minister, had been more interested in what had been found out at Cody's ranch than in their coffee and donuts.

With a shrug, Cody had deferred all the questions to her and her dad, as if he'd somehow known it wasn't smart to comment on an ongoing investigation. Fortunately her father knew that as well, so he didn't share her speculation with the other parishioners. Nobody knew anything beyond that a body had been found; they didn't even know if it was a man or a woman. And they definitely didn't know that she believed that person had been murdered.

Bethany wanted to keep it that way as long as she could. She'd wanted to share as few details as possible because to her, everyone was a possible suspect. Even Cody...

Though she didn't want him to be. Once she got home,

she would look up at that coverage of the rodeo. She would, hopefully, confirm that Theresa Muldoon was alive. But then who was dead?

Cody's mother? The gossip around town had always been that she'd run off with a ranch hand. Feeling sorry for Cody over that had been one of the first things that had drawn Bethany to him, but Cody had been so strong and smart and funny that he hadn't wanted or needed anyone's pity. He wasn't just a survivor; he was a success.

But what had become of his mother? Had she started her life over somewhere else? Or had it actually ended all those years ago on the ranch?

Bethany should have collected a DNA sample from Cody. She'd brought a kit with her, but she hadn't wanted to take the time then. Or risk the closeness to him—not with how he'd been affecting her. Seeing his love for his daughter tonight had flooded Bethany with feelings she had no business feeling. With a warmth. With longing.

Maybe it was just being back here, in Bear Creek, that was making her feel like a lovesick teenager again. She had a career now, all the things she'd always wanted… but Cody.

She didn't have Cody.

And if she wasn't careful, she might not have a career. She'd done a video walk-through with the police officer who'd responded to the break-in at her apartment. Nothing had been missing. While she didn't have a lot of jewelry, it hadn't been touched. Her TV hadn't been either. So what had someone been after?

Her?

She'd had plenty of threats since the arrest of the serial killer. What was wrong with the world that people could actually idolize a murderer? He wasn't Robin Hood. He hadn't taken from the rich to give to the poor. He'd just taken lives, cutting them cruelly short. They'd tracked one of his fans from the DNA he'd left on his letters, but Jimmy Lee Howard hadn't done anything except send letters. So far...

Bethany glanced into her rearview mirror again and gasped at how close and bright the headlamps were now. The vehicle must have sped up, must have tried to catch her. She should have been the one catching it, stopping the driver to question why they'd been at the crime scene. What possible interest could anyone have in it?

Just idle curiosity?

She wished that was all it was. That there wasn't a killer in Bear Creek.

She wanted one place in the world to be as pure and untouched as Molly Shepard was. And if the killer was just someone who'd passed through town, then they were probably long gone and had no idea that their victim had been discovered.

So the killer would have no reason to return to the scene...

No reason to follow Bethany.

Wanting to know who was behind her, Bethany began to slow so she could pull to the shoulder of the narrow highway. But even though she slowed, the vehicle behind her didn't. It rammed into the rear corner of her SUV. She spun into the steep ditch on the side of the road. The front end struck first, the hood crumpling, metal screeching—and then the airbag exploded. It knocked her head back and into the side post. And everything went black.

The driver of the vehicle could not have planned what had happened as well as it had.

FBI agent Bethany Snow might be good at catching serial killers, but she had no defensive driving skills. She had done nothing to protect herself, to prevent that sheriff's department SUV from going into the ditch.

Had she even realized that she'd been followed?

That she was being watched?

She would know now...

If she survived the crash.

The driver backed up the vehicle they'd borrowed, one that had a big bumper on the front and the heavy metal carriage from a plow to protect it from crumpling, to make sure that it was strong enough to force an SUV off the road. It had easily done that.

One of the headlights was broken, though, and the glass in the road crunched beneath the tires as the driver eased a foot off the brake and edged forward, coming up closer to the SUV. It was hard to see into the ditch, into the vehicle, but there was no movement inside it.

Agent Snow must have been knocked unconscious... at least.

At most.

She did not survive.

Chapter Seven

Frustration and fear warred within Cody, making his stomach churn. He'd shut off the stove and headed out with Molly. He hadn't wanted to bring her with him in case he found something like he had the other night… like a body. But he couldn't leave her alone either.

He could have called the sheriff's office and asked for help finding his father and Sammy. But some people around town had already started asking if he thought he should put his dad somewhere, like one of their memory-care places. He didn't want to file a missing persons report for him and risk having social services get involved, taking his father away from him, taking his father away from the ranch. Leaving it would kill Don Shepard.

And Cody had already lost one parent.

To another man?

To another life?

Or to death?

He wasn't sure which scenario would make him feel

better. Probably none since it wouldn't change the fact that his mother was gone.

Where was his dad?

He drove all around the ranch, even out to the crime scene. Because he hadn't found Sammy's truck parked near any of the barns closer to the ranch house, he'd thought he might find it out here, where Cody had wanted to build a barn. Now he wasn't sure if he should disturb the ground any further, even once Bethany released the crime scene.

But all the reasons he'd wanted to build on this site were still the same. It was halfway between the ranch house and town. And had that well for water. It was far enough out that it could operate almost independently. While cattle would remain the focus on the Shepard Ranch, like his father wanted, out here Cody could breed and board and raise horses.

To start his own ranch…on the place where he and Bethany had shared so many of their dreams, dreams that had taken them in entirely different directions. And yet somehow they'd both wound up back here. Had that been some kind of divine intervention?

Or just a sad coincidence?

It had all felt so right in church this morning, and trimming the tree with Molly. It had felt like they were meant to be, like he'd always thought. But he'd thought wrong all those years ago. And he was undoubtedly wrong now.

Bethany hadn't been able to wait to get away from him earlier, just as she hadn't that night when she'd broken his heart here next to the old well on the property. He should have known better than to trust her with his heart after his mom left. Theresa had proved to be just as untrustworthy. He would be smarter to focus just on his family now. On Molly and his dad who needed him and would never hurt him like Bethany had when she'd dumped him.

He wasn't the only one who'd been dumped here. That poor person who'd been buried in the barrel had been dumped far more cruelly. Who could have done something like that?

And where were they now?

He hoped far from Bear Creek. He didn't want them anywhere near his daughter, his family...

Where was his father? His friend?

He stared through the windshield at the mound of dirt, at the yellow tape fluttering around the hole in the ground. Sammy's truck wasn't here. Wasn't anywhere on the ranch...

Maybe he'd gone to town for something and had thought it would be such a quick trip that he hadn't wanted to interrupt the tree trimming. Cody headed out that way, down the bumpy gravel road straight to the highway.

Maybe he should have called Bethany, asked her to help him find his father, but he didn't want her getting any more involved in his life than she already was. Because she was going to leave. He expected her to go. But not Sammy and his dad.

Anxious to find them, he pressed his boot down harder on the accelerator, and the pickup bounced up and down on the ruts and ridges in the old gravel road so much that he almost felt as if he was riding a bronco again. Usually he would have made some joke about it to Molly, and she would have giggled and raised up one arm like she was riding a bull.

But they both stayed silent. She was so empathetic that she must have felt his fear, his concern for his dad and his friend. The gravel ended on the shoulder of the highway, and he braked and contemplated which way to take.

While Cody had been searching the ranch property, Sammy might have taken this road from town back to the ranch. He could already be there. Or he might still be in town.

Cody pulled off the two-track, gravel spewing out from beneath his back tires, as he turned toward town. He wasn't sure why. It was likely that Sammy had headed back to the ranch already. But something compelled him to go this way.

To make sure…

But when he'd driven a few miles without even passing another vehicle, he reconsidered his decision. This was probably a waste of time. But here the road was too narrow, the ditches too steep for him to safely turn around the truck. So he continued on toward town, waiting until the road widened. But before it did, he noticed lights ahead…brake lights but they weren't directly in front of him, they were up, at an odd angle…and then he saw why as he drew closer. His heart slammed against his ribs as fear shot through him.

A vehicle had gone off into one of those steep ditches. It wasn't a pickup box sticking up, so it wasn't Sammy's truck. It was some kind of SUV.

How had it gone off the road? And why? The road wasn't snow covered and slippery. There hadn't been enough snow for that, just those few fat flakes drifting down every once in a while. So what had happened?

Maybe there'd been an animal in the road and the driver had swerved. Or maybe they'd been drinking or had fallen asleep behind the wheel...

As Cody slowed down and neared the SUV, the headlamps of his truck glinted off the broken glass in the road...from lights, from some kind of collision. He glanced around looking for the other vehicle, but there was just the one in the ditch. Had the other just driven off?

Cody couldn't do that. He had to check to see if anyone was still inside the SUV. And if they needed help, he would call 911. He braked in the road, put the truck in park and turned on his hazards.

"What happened, Daddy? Did that person have an accident?" Molly asked as she pointed through the windshield.

"I don't know what happened, but I'm going to find out," he said, reaching for the driver's door. Molly reached for her belt. "No, honey," he said. "You need to stay in here." In case anyone in the SUV was hurt, he didn't want her to see it, didn't want her to have any horrible images burned into her memory like he had the image of that skeleton burned in his. "I'll be right back."

"But, Daddy—"

"I *need* you to stay in the truck," he said. "I need to focus on whoever's in that SUV, and there might not be anyone in there." That could have been why the other vehicle left. The driver of the SUV might have hopped inside with them for a ride to town. That was the kind of thing that happened in Bear Creek. Instead of road rage and fights over traffic accidents, people helped each other…like everyone had been trying to help him with his daughter and his dad.

He pushed open the driver's door and stepped out onto the street, onto that broken glass. It must have been a big light from a big vehicle, but then it would've had to have been to knock the SUV off into the ditch like it had. Had that been an accident or intentional? He hurried over to the SUV, and as he got closer, he saw the sheriff's department logo on the side of it.

"No…" he managed through the fear choking him, making it hard to breathe, to move. This had to be the vehicle that Bethany had been driving. This was the route she would have taken from the ranch to town. His legs a little shaky, he hurried toward the front of the vehicle. It was crumpled into the ditch, the hood pushed up with steam escaping into the cool night air. The slope of the ditch was so steep that Cody's boots slipped, and he would have fallen if not for reaching out to grab the SUV, to lean against the side of it as he maneuvered to the driver's door. A deflated airbag covered most of the side window, so he couldn't see much inside the vehicle, just the shadow of someone slumped over the deflated bag on the steering wheel. Was it Bethany? His hand shaking, he pulled out his cell phone and pressed for an emergency call.

"911, what's your emergency?" the dispatcher asked.

"I'm on Highway 41 halfway between the town of Bear Creek and the Shepard Ranch, and I found a Bear Creek Sheriff Department SUV in a ditch. I think the sheriff's daughter, Bethany Snow, is trapped inside. Send help ASAP."

"Sir, what is your—"

He clicked off his cell, unwilling to stay on the line to answer questions right now, unwilling to leave Bethany trapped inside the vehicle. It could be smoke instead of steam rising from the engine. He pulled on the driver's door handle, but it didn't budge. It was locked. So he knocked on the glass, which was intact, but nobody stirred inside, the shadow remained slumped in the seat. Cody reached behind him for the handle of the rear door. It also didn't move.

To check her, to make sure she was all right, he was going to have to force his way inside. But how?

He tried pounding on that rear window; the glass shuddered but didn't break. He needed something sharp like those special weapons police officers used to break the glass on submerged vehicles. Fortunately it hadn't been raining and there was no water in the steep ditch, but with the way the steam was escaping the engine area, maybe it would have been better if there was. Then he wouldn't have had to worry about it catching fire.

The thought of that spurred his pulse into overdrive, and he scrambled around, looking for anything to break the window. He grabbed a rock. No. It was bigger than a rock. A piece of concrete that must have broken off a block or something being hauled.

He used the sharp edge of it against the window of the rear door. The glass spiderwebbed out from the point of impact. He kept slamming the concrete against the glass until the whole window collapsed. Then he reached through it and unlocked the door, which didn't open very far before stopping hard against the slope of the ditch. The front door probably wouldn't open at all, being between the ditch and the crumpled fender pushed against it.

He squeezed through that rear door and into the back seat. Fortunately no glass or mesh separated the back from the front, so he was able to lean over the console to where the driver lay against the wheel, her black hair splayed over the deflated airbag. "Bethany!" If she hadn't heard him breaking the glass, she was unconscious.

Or…

No. He couldn't even consider that. He reached for her, brushing her silky hair aside until he touched her throat. Her pulse beat, albeit slowly. Too slowly…

Was she breathing?

He leaned forward and the SUV shifted, slipping deeper into the ditch. Metal creaked as the hood crumpled more, and the door through which he'd squeezed moved. Then a small body appeared inside the opening.

"Daddy?" Molly called out, her voice querulous with tears and nerves. "What's going on? You were pounding…"

"Go back to the truck," he told her. He didn't want her around all the broken glass and twisted metal. He didn't want her getting hurt, too.

Because it was obvious that Bethany was hurt.

"Is that Miss Bethany?" she asked, her voice cracking with fear now as she peered over the seat at the dark-haired driver. "Is she okay?"

"Yes," he said, and he hoped he wasn't lying to his daughter.

"She's not moving, Daddy," Molly said. His little girl was smart and observant. "You're supposed to kiss her."

She must have been talking about CPR, about him giving Bethany mouth to mouth.

He moved his hand from Bethany's neck to her lips, and he felt the faint brush of her breath against his skin. "She's breathing," he assured his worried daughter. "You need to get back up to the road and into the truck. Help is coming." And not a moment too soon.

Bethany was breathing but her breathing was soft and shallow. Did she have internal injuries? Where was that ambulance? He'd thought they would come quickly since he'd said it was a sheriff's department SUV.

"Daddy, you're supposed to kiss her," Molly insisted as she backed away from the SUV. "That's what the prince does when Snow White is sleeping."

If he'd thought it was necessary or that it would work for Bethany to regain consciousness, he would gladly kiss her. He sucked in a breath as he realized that he wanted to kiss her, but only if she was conscious and if she wanted him to.

But he couldn't think about that now; all he'd think about was saving her and praying that she would wake up. "Please, God," he whispered.

The whine of sirens drew Bethany out of oblivion, back to consciousness. Her head pounded, not with the noise, but with pain. She flinched at the intensity of it, and a moan slipped through her lips.

"Miss Bethany..." came a small voice.

Someone touched her cheek, pushing back her hair... a small hand. Panic gripped her heart. Was Molly with her? Was she hurt too? Concern for the child jerked Bethany fully conscious, and she lifted her head from the gurney on which she was lying in what appeared to be the back of an ambulance. "What are you doing here?" she asked. "What happened?"

Molly hadn't been with her. Bethany had left the ranch alone. But she hadn't been alone for long on the highway before someone had pulled onto the road behind her, from the two-track that led back to the old homestead, back to the crime scene...

Had that vehicle been Cody's? But he wouldn't have driven her off the road. He wouldn't have done anything to endanger Bethany's life, and he especially wouldn't have done anything to endanger his daughter.

"Where's your daddy?" Bethany asked.

Molly waved outside the open ambulance doors where Cody stood with the paramedics and a couple of state police troopers. "He's telling them how we found you in the ditch."

"What were you doing out?" Bethany asked.

"We were looking for Grandpa and Sammy."

The last Bethany remembered they'd been in the kitchen. But a long time had passed from when she'd arrived at Shepherd Ranch to when they'd finished decorating the tree. Hours. She'd arrived midafternoon and had left after dark; of course, it got dark earlier this time of year. Apparently while she and Cody and Molly had been preoccupied with the tree, Sammy and Don Shepard had slipped off somewhere. Where? The old homestead?

"Did you find them?" Bethany asked.

Molly shook her head, and her strawberry blond curls bounced around her shoulders. "No. I hope they're not in a ditch, too."

Bethany wondered about that, wondered if they were the ones who'd put her here. But before she could ask any more questions, voices got louder as the first responders returned to the ambulance.

"We'll get her to the ER for a CT scan right away, Mr. Shepard," one of the men addressed Cody, who hovered just outside those open doors.

"Molly?" he called out to his daughter. "You need to get down. You need to let them check out Miss Bethany."

"She's awake, Daddy! Miss Bethany is awake."

Cody released a ragged-sounding sigh. "Thank God."

"Daddy was praying real hard for you to wake up," Molly shared. "I guess that works the same as a kiss…"

Bethany's mother always spoke of the healing powers of prayer, but Bethany's own faith had begun to slip over the last several years. She'd seen too many horrors, too much tragedy and loss. But that morning, in church, she'd felt so at peace.

And now…

She couldn't deny that Cody's prayers had worked. She was sore and her head hurt, but she knew she wasn't hurt too badly. It could have been worse, so much worse. So maybe God was watching over her, just as her mother had always said. And maybe God had sent Cody Shepard and his sweet little daughter to rescue her.

But who had put her in the ditch? From whom was she in danger? Cody's father and Molly's nanny?

Or someone else…

Someone who might have found something in her apartment and realized where she'd gone.

Home to Bear Creek…and followed her here.

Chapter Eight

Once the paramedics had assured him that Bethany wasn't seriously hurt, Cody had buckled Molly into her booster seat to head back home. Bethany's dad and mom had showed up at the scene, too, and despite Bethany's assurances that she was fine, they'd insisted on her getting checked out at the ER. So with her dad protecting her and investigating the accident, Bethany didn't need Cody. But his father did.

Where had his dad and Sammy gone?

With the ambulance and the other vehicles heading toward town, Cody had turned back to the ranch. As he'd hoped, he found Sammy's truck parked in its usual spot near the kitchen door. He felt only a faint twinge of guilt that he checked the front bumper and the light—and breathed a sigh of relief when he'd found them unscathed.

If only Bethany had been the same. But she'd had a bump swelling on the side of her head from the post between the doors. That airbag hadn't deployed right away, not like the one from the steering wheel. That was probably why she'd lost consciousness.

But she could have lost more than that.

She could have lost her life.

He found himself reaching out for Sammy's truck, settling his hand onto the hood. It was still warm. They hadn't been back long.

Molly had unclasped her belt and wriggled out of her booster seat and the passenger's door of his truck. "Daddy, they're back!" she exclaimed, and she rushed up the couple of steps to the back door and pushed it open. "Sammy!"

Cody vaulted the steps and followed her into the kitchen where Sammy was back at the stove like he'd been that afternoon. Almost acting as if he'd never left.

"Sammy," Molly said again until the older man turned toward her. "We just found Miss Bethany in the ditch!"

Sammy's brow furrowed beneath the long white hair falling across it. "What are you talking about?" he asked with confusion.

"Miss Bethany was in the ditch, and she was sleeping. But Daddy wouldn't kiss her to wake her up like Snow White. But we prayed real hard, and she woke up. And then the ambulance came and her mommy and daddy and everybody was really happy and really sad at the same time." Her voice cracked now, reminding Cody how scared his daughter had been. How attached she'd already gotten to Bethany.

Seeing Bethany like that, unconscious and trapped in the crash… Emotions overwhelmed him and made him realize that *he* was still as attached to Bethany as he'd always been, even though he knew she wasn't staying in Bear Creek. He always knew she wasn't staying.

While he'd changed his mind about that, while he'd changed, she hadn't, at least in that respect. She might have become even more focused on her career than she'd been when she'd left town. He couldn't deny that it was an impressive career doing important things. In catching that killer, she'd probably saved countless lives.

Knowing tonight she could have lost her own had pain and fear gripping his heart so hard that he struggled for a breath. He forced himself to inhale deeply and focus on his daughter, on assuaging her fears. "Molly, Miss Bethany is going to be all right," he said. "Now you should check on Snowball and make sure she hasn't knocked down the Christmas tree."

Molly nodded and took off running toward the living room.

"How'd the FBI lady go in the ditch?" Sammy asked. "The roads aren't slippery now."

"No, they're not," Cody agreed. "Which you would know since you must have got back just before us. Where have you been? We were out looking for you and Dad when we found Bethany."

Sammy sighed and pushed a big hand through his long hair. "Your dad took off somewhere while you and Molly were busy with the tree. So I got in my truck and went looking for him."

Cody's brow furrowed now as confusion and doubts gripped him. "He couldn't have gotten that far that you couldn't have caught him on foot."

"I have a lot more years of aches and pains than you do, Cody. And…" Sammy's face flushed, and he added,

"I think he was already gone for a while by the time I noticed that he wasn't in the house. I'd just figured he'd gone back to his room. But when I went to check on him…"

Cody glanced at the table where that plate had been sitting with the untouched sandwich. It was gone now. Would his dad have gone back to his suite without eating? Would Sammy have let him?

"I'm sorry," Sammy murmured.

"Where'd you find him?" Cody asked.

"Uh-uh…"

Alarm gripped Cody. "You *did* find him?"

"When I looked everywhere that I could think to look and hadn't found him, I came back to the house to tell you and see if you wanted to call the police, and he was sitting on the porch," Sammy said.

"Oh, thank God…" Relief and gratitude for His help for the second time tonight surged through Cody.

Sammy continued, "And then you were gone…"

"I got worried when I couldn't find you guys and you wouldn't answer your cell," Cody said. And he wondered why Sammy hadn't responded to any of his calls.

Sammy pulled open one of the drawers of the kitchen cabinets. "I put it in here and must have forgotten all about it."

"I called from the kitchen a couple of times," Cody said, "and I didn't hear it ring…" Was his friend lying to him? But why?

Because he hadn't gone after Cody's dad but after Bethany Snow? What reason would he have? And how could he have done it without damaging his own vehicle? Unless he'd used one of the others on the ranch.

There were several trucks parked around the barns, used to deliver feed to the cattle or to plow the roads on the property.

Sammy held up the phone to Cody, showing all those missed calls. And the silencer on. "I must have hit that button without realizing it."

Still, Cody couldn't help but worry and wonder how well he knew his old friend. Despite all the years they'd spent on the circuit together, Cody didn't know much about the man's personal life. Sammy had never talked much about himself, but Cody had just figured that was his personality. Stoic—like Cody's father had always been.

Maybe that was why Cody had been so drawn to the older man: because Sammy had reminded him of his dad. And like Don Shepard, Sammy had done his best to protect Cody. The former rodeo clown had rescued him many times from a rampaging bull or a bronc. So Cody had trusted him with his life, with his daughter and with his dad.

But could he trust him with Bethany's life?

Was there some reason that Sammy wanted the FBI agent out of the picture?

Bethany's head pounded, more now with exhaustion and frustration than because of the slight concussion she had. If only she could have convinced her mother that she wasn't seriously hurt.

But her mom had insisted on helping Bethany straight to her room to rest after they'd returned from the ER, which had made Bethany feel like a child again instead of the capable FBI agent that she was. Especially after she'd allowed her mother to tuck her into her bed when she should have been back at the crash site searching for any evidence that might lead her to the identity of the hit-and-run driver who'd forced her into the ditch.

She wanted to question Molly's nanny. To find out where he and Cody's father had really been when Cody had been concerned enough that they'd disappeared to go running around to find them. Fortunately for her, Cody had been out and about, or she might have frozen to death in that crumpled SUV. While it was a mild winter so far in Montana, it was still cold enough that she could have been seriously injured or died from exposure alone. Not to mention that that hit-and-run driver might have returned to make sure she didn't survive if Cody hadn't been there.

With as upset as Bethany's mother had been at the crash site and hospital, Bethany hadn't wanted to worry her anymore, so she hadn't argued with her. But once her mom had left her room, Bethany called to check in with her bureau chief. She told him about the break-in at her house and about the hit-and-run this evening and asked him to step up his search for Jimmy Lee Howard.

A gasp drew her attention to the doorway where her father stood, eavesdropping. She felt a flash of concern, followed quickly by relief that it had been her father, and not her mother, who'd overheard her conversation. As if he was worried about the same thing, her dad stepped into her bedroom and closed the door.

Bethany quickly wrapped up her call to focus on him. Once again she was struck by how much older he looked. The wrinkles were more defined in his face, and there were dark circles beneath his eyes. "Are you all right?" she asked with concern.

"I came up here to ask you that," he said. "And to apologize for getting you involved in this investigation. I didn't think…"

"Don't," she said. "Don't apologize. And don't worry about me."

"But someone broke into your place in Chicago? You've had threats?"

She nodded. "That's just part of the job," she said. The part she liked least about it. And then, for a moment, she struggled to remember what she liked most about it. She'd thought it would be the accolades. But she'd quickly grown tired of reporters and had no interest in getting any more attention for herself or for killers. She'd wanted to focus solely on the victims. But their families hadn't wanted that. They'd just wanted to live their lives and deal privately with their grief.

"Your mom worries about you," her dad said. "All the time. I thought she was being silly, overprotective, but now…" He shuddered. "Now I realize she was right to worry and to pray for you like she does."

Those prayers might have protected her tonight, the ones her mom had said and the ones Molly claimed that Cody had uttered while waiting for the ambulance. A twinge of regret struck her heart that he hadn't come to the hospital with her or at least showed up later to check on her. But he had his daughter with him, and Molly had already been upset. He'd also had to find his dad. Now she felt a pang of guilt that she'd been more concerned about herself than she'd been about him, about everything he had to deal with. She needed to call Cody to see if he'd found his dad and make sure they were all safe.

But her dad lingered in her bedroom, leaning against the closed door as if he couldn't stand without the support, or maybe he was trying to block out every threat to her safety. He couldn't do that. Nobody could.

"Mom's prayers work," Bethany said. "I'm fine. I'm only lying down in order to appease her."

"In order for *me* to appease her, I'd have to take back that case from you," he said. "She thinks that's what put you in danger."

Bethany shrugged. "I don't know if she's right about that. It's certainly not the only reason I could be in danger."

He grimaced. "I hate that your job puts you in danger."

She shrugged again. "It doesn't matter what a person does for a living, they can come across someone evil, like that school teacher–serial killer, or they might just be in the wrong place at the wrong time. Then there are the people whose domestic partners have hurt or killed them…" She wondered which circumstance had resulted in the death of the woman whose remains Cody had uncovered at the ranch, at their special place. "You know there's no way to protect everyone from danger."

"You can get the bad guys off the street, like you do," he said, his voice husky with emotion. "I really admire you, Beth. I hate that you're in danger. But I really admire what you do, how determined you've always been to protect the innocent, to put away the guilty."

She wished her reasons had always been as altruistic as he made them sound. But she'd also wanted so badly to gain his respect, to excel in the field he'd chosen—law enforcement. "You're the one I've always admired, Dad," she said softly. "The one I always wanted to be like."

He snorted and shook his head. "Your mom is the far better person of the two of us," he said. "The stronger one, the smarter one, the more spiritual one…"

Maybe Sally Snow had, with her prayers, protected Bethany from further harm than she could have been in. She smiled and nodded. "The scarier one since we're both up here hiding from her," she pointed out.

He chuckled. "I'll let her know that you're fine," he said.

"I'll come down in a minute," Bethany said. But she wanted to make that call first. She waited until her father levered himself wearily away from her door and stepped out into the hall. Then she dialed another contact on her cell, one she'd taken off the police report from when the body had been found on the Shepard Ranch.

"Hello?" he answered.

"Cody."

"Bethany! Are you all right?" he asked anxiously.

"Yes, I'm fine," she said.

"Really? Your mother said you have a concussion."

"You talked to my mother?" she asked.

"I called to check on you, to make sure you were all right," he said.

Warmth flooded her heart that he'd been concerned. When she'd met Cody Shepard all those years ago, he'd been a sweet boy; now he was a good man. A really good one.

"I should have called to check on you," she said, shoving down her guilt.

"Why? I'm fine."

"Did you find your dad?"

"He was here." He sighed.

"And Sammy?" she asked.

"He was, too."

She wanted to ask if there had been any damage to his vehicle, but she knew she'd upset Cody before with her suspicion and her questions.

"His truck was fine," he said, as if he'd read her mind. "Not a scratch on it. And he'd left his phone in the kitchen drawer."

She wanted to ask if he believed his friend, but she could hear something in his voice that suggested he might not. She intended to check out Sammy Felton, to make sure he was safe for Cody and his daughter to be around. That guilt she'd felt before struck again like a slap across her face as she realized *she* might not be safe for Cody and Molly to be around. If someone had followed her to Bear Creek determined to harm her, Cody or Molly could get hurt in the cross fire. Or her mother and father...

"And your dad?" she asked. "He's all right?"

"He must have been out wandering around the ranch like he sometimes does," Cody said. "He found his way back before Sammy and Molly and I all did."

"He didn't get too cold?" she asked from beneath the mound of blankets her mother had piled on her. All the covers hadn't warmed her up as much as the sound of Cody's deep voice rumbling in her ear.

"He's fine," he said. "Thank you."

"Thank you," she said, "for finding me." She had no idea how long it might have taken for someone else to come along. That part of the highway wasn't well traveled. There wasn't much out that way except Cody's ranch.

So who had been out at the old homestead? Had someone been at the crime scene making sure they'd left nothing behind to incriminate themselves? Or had they just accidentally stumbled across that gravel road to wait on her, to catch her returning to town?

She'd already asked the bureau chief to track down that fan of the serial killer, to make sure Jimmy Lee Howard hadn't taken a trip to Montana. But until she knew if he had, she had to back away from Cody and his daughter. She couldn't put them in danger. He already had too much to deal with on his own. He didn't need her adding any more difficulty or danger to his life.

Without saying anything else to him, she disconnected the call. She cut off the temptation to keep listening to his deep voice, to lose herself in the memory of how his green eyes had always glittered when he'd looked at her, of how his mouth had always curved into that beguiling grin…until she'd broken his heart. Cody had already been through too much in life. She had to protect him from any more pain as a result of her.

Chapter Nine

Feeling like an anxious teenager again, Cody stood outside the Snows' kitchen door. It had been a week since he'd seen Bethany, since she'd trimmed the tree with him and Molly. He was worried about her, but this morning in church, her mother had assured him Bethany was fine. She'd been up and around the house just an hour after the crash and hadn't even had much of a headache.

So why had she sent someone else out to get his DNA the Monday morning after the crash? Why hadn't she called again since that night she'd checked to see if he'd found his dad and Sammy? Why hadn't she been in church that morning?

He hadn't wanted to interrogate her mother since Mrs. Snow was always kind to him and helped so much with Molly. That was why he stood at her door now, with Molly trembling with excitement next to him. In church that morning, Mrs. Snow had asked if Molly would be interested in helping her make the Christmas cookies she made every year, which she shared at church and gave out to all the neighbors. The woman was the most generous and genuine person Cody had ever met. And he imagined having his four-year-old daughter's help was going to make more work for the sweet woman, not alleviate any of it, so he'd offered to help out as well.

And if he was able to see Bethany…

Then he might be able to find out why she'd been avoiding him. Had she talked to Theresa? Had Theresa said something bad about him? He doubted it with as badly as Theresa had felt when she'd told him she didn't love him, that she didn't think she ever really had. Maybe it was out of guilt that she'd signed away her parental rights. He would have rather shared Molly with her than have his daughter's mother give her up. He knew what that felt like having your mother abandon you.

And undoubtedly, when those DNA results came back, that was what Bethany would confirm had happened to him. Maybe she already had and that was why she'd been avoiding him. Because if she'd proved the skeleton was his mom, surely the FBI agent would have been back to the ranch, asking more questions, maybe even searching the property.

He shuddered at the thought just as the door opened.

"Oh, no!" Mrs. Snow exclaimed. "You must have been standing there so long that you've gotten chilled. Come in! Come in!" She reached out for his arm and for Molly, tugging them both into the warmth of her home, the warmth of her presence.

Clearly she'd already been baking because Cody breathed in the scent of vanilla, cinnamon and nutmeg, as well as a hint of almond and peppermint.

"Mmm…" Molly hummed appreciatively. "It smells yummy in here."

"I started with the boring cookies like the snicker-doodles, peppermint bark and almond crescents and saved the fun sugar cookies for us to cut out and deco-rate."

"Yay!" Molly exclaimed. "We get to cut cookies? And will we use sprinkles to decorate them?"

"We'll make frosting in every color and then put the sprinkles on."

Molly clapped her mittened hands together with ex-citement.

Cody's heart swelled with the joy his daughter took in the simplest of things. She was such a happy, hope-ful child, and she made him so very happy and even hopeful. Mrs. Snow was still holding his arm and she squeezed it and smiled at him, as if she knew exactly what he was feeling and she felt it, too.

"Let's take off our coats and get to work," she said. As Molly pulled off her mittens and unzipped her jacket, Mrs. Snow leaned closer to Cody. "She's such a special little girl. You're doing an amazing job with her, Cody Shepard."

Tears stung his eyes with gratitude that the woman he'd always considered the best parent he'd known was praising his parenting. "Thank you, Mrs. Snow. Coming from you…" Emotion choked him, making his voice so gruff that he had to clear his throat. "Well, that means so much."

Mrs. Snow blinked her eyes and smiled at him. "You're a special man, Cody Shepard," she said. "I've always thought so."

If only her daughter shared that opinion of him.

Instead, he worried that Bethany had stayed away from him this past week because she'd begun to suspect him again. Did she think he'd killed Theresa and buried her on the ranch, and then, with his daughter in his truck, driven Bethany off the road? His stomach churned as he felt physically sick that she could think that little of him. But he didn't know what upset him more—that she didn't know him, or that she'd become so cynical she suspected everyone was capable of evil.

"What do you think, Bethany?" Mrs. Snow asked.

Cody blinked to clear his vision and peered around the big kitchen, and he found her standing at the bottom of the stairwell that came down into the kitchen from the second story. Their gazes met, but before he could identify the emotion shimmering in her blue eyes, she quickly looked away, down at his daughter who rushed up and wrapped her arms around Bethany's waist.

"Miss Bethany!" Molly exclaimed. "I missed you!"

Now he realized what emotion he'd glimpsed in Bethany's eyes: fear. She'd often said how uncomfortable she was around kids. That was why she'd worked with Roberta at her practice rather than babysat like her sister had. But his daughter was clearly falling for her anyway after just a few meetings. He could easily understand Molly's devotion to Bethany's mom; everybody had wanted Mrs. Snow to be their mother— no one more than Cody. But Bethany wasn't anything like her mother.

If she was still uncomfortable around children, maybe that was her appeal to Molly, like cats seemed drawn to people who didn't like them. He often found

Snowball in his bed, curled up against his back or on his pillow pressed against his head instead of sleeping with Molly. Not that he didn't like Snowball. But he'd always preferred bigger animals, like horses and bulls.

Bethany had preferred animals to children. She'd often said she didn't want kids of her own. But if that had been fear he'd seen in her eyes, it wasn't about Molly because Bethany wrapped her arms around his little girl and hugged her close. It might have been about the other night, about the hit-and-run. And he didn't blame her for being frightened about that; he was scared for her.

"Are you going to make cookies with us?" Molly asked. "Daddy's going to help, too."

"Daddy bakes?" Bethany asked, and she met his gaze again over his daughter's head.

Over the past four years of Molly's life, he'd learned things to do for and with her that would enforce their bond. Baking was one of them. "I'm nowhere near your mother's level," he said. "But I can bake up a batch of premixed cookie dough like nobody's business."

"I told you he was special," her mother murmured.

"Daddy's the best daddy ever!" Molly declared.

His heart swelled with love and pride. But he smiled and shook his head in protest. "Shh, we don't want Mr. Snow to hear you say that. He might toss us out of his house."

Molly's eyes widened with shock, and she pressed a hand over her mouth. "Oh, no. I don't want him to feel bad."

Mrs. Snow laughed and swatted at Cody's shoulder. "Don't tease her. Nobody's throwing anybody out," she said. Turning to Molly, she added, "And Mr. Snow certainly wouldn't feel bad about you loving your dad like you do. And he can't argue with you either since he's never baked a cookie in his life, has he, Bethany?"

She shook her head, and her black hair moved like silk around her shoulders. He knew it felt like silk, too; he hadn't been able to appreciate that when he'd been brushing it back from her face, when he'd been feeling for her pulse.

He winced as he relived those awful moments. He had so much already to worry about with Molly and his dad and the ranch, he couldn't worry about her, too. He couldn't let himself fall for her all over again. If he was smart, he'd make some excuse and rush Molly out of there or at least leave himself to clear his head and to steel his heart.

Bethany doubted her mother had invited Molly and Cody over because she actually needed help baking cookies. Sally Snow was playing matchmaker and not too subtly either since she'd prodded Bethany into admitting that Cody was special. He had always been special, but now he was even more so since he'd taken on all the responsibilities as a father, as a caregiver to his father and as the business manager of his family ranch. Also as the man who'd come to her rescue the week before. She cringed to think what might have happened if the hit-and-run driver had come back while he and his daughter were there.

They might have been hurt, too, because of her.

She worried about that now. That was why she hadn't gone to church that morning even though she'd missed it, more than she'd thought she would've. She'd missed Cody and Molly, too.

More than she should have…

Her mother had always been so empathetic to the emotions and moods of those around her that she'd probably either picked up on Bethany missing them or on Molly missing her. She should have told her mother about her concerns, that danger might have followed her home to Bear Creek. But she hadn't wanted to worry her any more than she already was.

Even though DNA from the letters had identified the serial killer's most ardent fan as Jimmy Lee Howard, nobody had been able to locate him. Chicago was a big city with a lot of places to hide, though Bethany would have expected him to be found in his mother's basement. He hadn't been there or at any of the local fleabag motels he'd stayed at when his mother had kicked him out before because he'd hurt her animals or her.

Was he the one trying to hurt Bethany now?

And would he harm anyone who got too close to her, who meant too much to her?

Cody and Molly were beginning to mean too much to her. And that was why, when Molly implored her to bake with them, Bethany couldn't bring herself to refuse.

If only she could have claimed she was working…

But until the DNA results came back, she had no leads about the identity of the woman found on the ranch. While Theresa Muldoon hadn't called her back, Bethany had watched that rodeo footage of her recent competition. The woman was alive and well.

Unlike that skeleton.

The coroner hadn't been able to pinpoint her time of death, just that she'd been buried a long time. The initial forensics done on the barrel and clothing had confirmed that as well. Hopefully when the results of the more extensive tests came back, they would pinpoint how long the barrel and the woman had been in the ground. Twenty years?

That was how long ago Cody's mother was rumored to have left Bear Creek, when he'd been ten. Maybe that was why he'd always seemed so drawn to Bethany's mother, even more so than to his stepmom. Roberta wasn't the nurturing kind, not like Sally Snow. Roberta was always so busy that it was difficult for her to give the undivided attention that Bethany's mom gave to people, but she'd always listened to Bethany and given great advice.

Sally was busy now, helping Molly roll and cut cookies out of dough. Then she bustled around the kitchen, pulling cookie trays from her double ovens, while Cody, Molly and Bethany decorated the ones that had already cooled.

"Are you feeding all of Bear Creek?" Bethany asked her mom.

Sally chuckled and shook her head. "Good heavens, no, not with all the people moving into the area or back home like Cody and Molly." She looked at Bethany, pointedly, like she wanted her to move back, too. But she knew about the offer of the promotion, of the relocation to New York City. Fortunately, she didn't know about the danger. About the break-in.

As for the hit-and-run, Bethany and her father had done their best to downplay it as an accident, had suggested that the driver had had too much to drink, and when they'd seen the police logo on the SUV, they hadn't dared to stop. She and her dad had checked with all the repair shops and auto supply places in town, but they hadn't found anyone who'd taken a truck in for front-end damage or purchased a headlamp recently. So if that vehicle was still out there somewhere, it was driving around with just one light.

"That's a lot of frosting," Cody remarked, his deep voice pulling her from her thoughts.

She'd thought he was talking to his daughter, but he gestured at the Santa cookie that she'd liberally frosted.

"I like frosting," Molly said in her defense.

Bethany smiled at the little girl. "But I should probably save some for the other Santa Claus cookies," Bethany said.

"And for us!" Molly swiped her finger into the bowl and licked it.

Cody chuckled that deep chuckle that made Bethany's skin tingle at just the sound of it. "You don't need any frosting to make you sweeter," he said. But he dipped his finger into the bowl of green frosting and swiped it across his daughter's little nose.

She giggled and crossed her eyes trying to stare down at it. And Cody laughed harder.

At the sounds of their happiness, Bethany's heart ached as if it was expanding beyond its capacity. She had decided long ago she didn't have the capacity for this, for a home, for a family.

She'd always known she was more like her father, that she could focus only on her career, like he had when she was growing up. If he hadn't been off on a deployment, he'd been working a shift at the sheriff's office. Like he was now. She suspected the only case he was working now was hers. Looking for that vehicle that had struck her.

Molly wiped frosting from the end of her cute little nose. Then she licked her finger clean.

And Cody chuckled again.

Cody had brought his daughter back to Bear Creek because he'd thought it would be a good, safe place to raise her. If Bethany put either of them in danger, he would never forgive her. She needed to tell him the truth.

"Hey, Mom," she said as she jumped up from the kitchen table. "Can you take over the decorating with Molly for a minute?"

Her mother turned away from the oven she'd just switched off, and disappointment pulled the smile from her mouth. "Are you leaving?"

"No." Not yet but she intended to. "I need to talk to Cody in the living room."

"Uh-oh, Daddy," Molly muttered. "You're in trouble for putting that frosting on my nose."

Cody smiled. "You think Miss Bethany is putting me in a time-out?" he asked.

Her green eyes wide, she gave him a solemn nod. "Yup. You're not supposed to play with your food. That's what Sammy always says."

"I'm not going to argue with Sammy," Cody said with a shudder.

Was he faking that shudder? Just joking around? Or did his friend intimidate him? He was so big and silent. So disapproving, he had seemed, with Bethany. Why? What was Sammy Felton's story? She hadn't found one yet. She hadn't found much trace of a Sammy Felton at all. And she wondered if that was even his real name.

"I'm not going to argue with Miss Bethany either," Cody added, but he rose slowly from the table while she waited in the doorway between the kitchen and the dining room.

When he was finally heading her way, she crossed the dining room to the living room. Stockings hung from the fireplace mantel, a tree stood in the corner and a miniature Christmas village sat in the bay window. Her mother went all out for Christmas and not just with her baking. Presents overflowed the space already. Not just presents for family, but gifts that her mother had been collecting, and probably buying, to give out to those in need. Those who couldn't afford to have the Christmases that Bethany had always had, that she'd taken for granted.

Just like she'd taken her mother for granted.

In the little over a week that she'd been home, her mother had been out of the house more than Bethany's father had. She was busy teaching preschool at the church school, decorating the town square, collecting and buying and wrapping the gifts for the poor. No wonder everybody had wanted her for their mother; she was so generous and tireless.

"So am I in a time-out?" Cody asked.

While she'd been studying the room, Cody had been studying her; she'd felt his gaze on her. And her skin tingled as if he'd touched her, or maybe just because she wanted him to touch her…like he used to. Brushing her hair from her face, holding her hand… But she couldn't let him get any closer to her than he already was.

Not now. Not ever.

She wasn't staying. There was nothing for her to do in Bear Creek. She wasn't a preschool teacher or a baker. While she didn't always like the ugliness involving the crimes she investigated, she did like to serve and protect people, whether they appreciated it or not.

Now she needed to protect Cody and his daughter.

"You're not in a time-out," she said. "Your time is up."

His brow furrowed. "What?"

"You need to leave," she said. "You and Molly need to leave."

Cody's long, lean body stiffened. "Your mother invited us here," he said. "Even though you don't trust me, she does."

"I do, too," she admitted.

"Then why haven't you been back out to the ranch?"

"You wanted me there?" she wondered.

His face flushed, and he shrugged. "I thought you were investigating what Bruce, the excavator, found out there. I need to get back to work, but you haven't even released the crime scene yet."

"I have been back out to the scene," she said. And she hadn't found anything else, anything that the state crime techs had missed, although she did suspect that whoever had driven her off the road might have been there. The yellow tape had been ripped down. The wind might have done that. Or maybe even Cody, out of frustration.

"You can get back to building your barn," she told him.

He glanced out the window where snow was beginning to fall, so heavily that it looked more like night than late afternoon. But then the sun set so early now—

if it was even visible at all. He sighed. "Hopefully there's still time to dig the footings and pour the concrete."

"I'm sorry," she said. She should have released the scene earlier; she would have if she'd trusted herself to talk to him again. But while the headache from the concussion was gone, she still felt weaker and more vulnerable than she'd felt in a long time. She suspected that had less to do with the concussion than with Cody. If only the concussion could have taken away all her memories of him…

But then it probably wouldn't have mattered because now there was Molly. And Bethany was making new memories with her.

"It's not your fault someone buried that body out there," he said. His throat moved as if he was struggling hard to swallow and, his voice gruff, he asked, "Did you get the results back on that DNA yet? Do you know who she is?"

She shook her head. "I'm rushing it. I should know soon."

He drew in a deep breath and nodded. "That'll be good. Then you'll know it has nothing to do with the ranch…with my family."

"I want to believe that," she admitted. But she had her doubts.

"You are so cynical now," he muttered. "Did you finally accept that it's not Theresa? That I didn't bury my ex-wife there?"

"I saw the rodeo," she said. "The interviews afterward. It's not her."

"But you still want me out of here?" he asked. "What are you afraid of?"

"I'm not afraid of you," she said. Although she wondered if that was a lie. No. She wasn't afraid of Cody but of what he made her feel. She continued, "I'm afraid *for* you and for Molly."

His brow furrowed again. "Why?"

"I have concerns about Molly's nanny," she admitted.

Instead of leaping to his friend's defense as he had before, Cody's face flushed, and he looked away from her, out the window where the snow was falling heavily. "Sammy would never hurt me or Molly," he assured her.

He did seem to adore them, so maybe that was true, and maybe that was why the man was so reserved with her. He was worried she might hurt Cody or Molly. She was concerned about that, too. "I don't want you two getting hurt. That's why I've stayed away from the ranch. Why I didn't go to church, why you need to leave here…"

"What are you talking about?" he asked.

"I think it's possible someone followed me to Bear Creek," she confided, and she peered out the window, too, at the street. If anyone had followed her to town, it would be easy for them to learn where she lived. Everybody in Bear Creek knew where Sheriff and Mrs. Snow lived.

"Who would have followed you?" he asked. "Do you have a stalker? An ex-boyfriend who won't leave you alone?"

She chuckled softly. While she'd dated over the years, she hadn't had anyone she really could have called a boyfriend since Cody. She didn't want her personal life to stand in the way of professional advancement. She wanted to be free to take opportunities as they were offered. "No. But not everyone was happy I caught that serial killer."

"Of course he would have been upset that you stopped him," Cody said. "But he's in prison. He's never getting out."

"He has fans," she admitted with a heavy sigh. "At least one that we know of and whom some other agents are trying to track down for me." Could he be here? Would he have taken his fandom as far as trying to kill her to avenge his hero like he'd threatened? She couldn't take the risk. "That's why you and Molly need to stay away from me. I don't want to put you in danger."

Through the falling snow, she took notice of a vehicle parked at the curb a little way down the block. Smoke emanated from its exhaust, so it was running. It had been running for a while, a dark shadow behind the steering wheel of the steamed-up windshield. And as the sky darkened, the automatic headlamps suddenly came on.

Headlamp.

Just one of them came on.

Just one of them worked.

Her heart began to pound harder, faster.

"No. Stay here..." she murmured.

Had the driver seen them at the window? She stepped back slowly and turned toward the dining room. When she'd come downstairs and found Molly and Cody in the kitchen, she'd set her purse atop a kitchen cabinet that was too high for Molly to reach. She rushed to it now, grabbed it and reached inside for her holstered weapon. "Mom, stay in the house with Molly and Cody. Stay here, and call Dad. Tell him that I spotted the truck outside."

"Beth—" her mother began, her voice high with nerves.

But Bethany was already heading out the door. Or she would have been had a strong hand not gripped her arm and held her back. "You can't go out there alone!" Cody protested.

"This is what I do," she said. "Stay here with your daughter, with Mom." Then she tugged out of his grasp and slammed the door shut in his face as she left the house and these people she wanted to protect so badly.

She only hoped that it wasn't too late, that she hadn't already risked their lives as she was risking hers now to save them.

Chapter Ten

The slam of the door echoed throughout the suddenly quiet kitchen. Cody couldn't just stand there baking cookies while the woman he…the woman he used to love rushed off to confront someone who might be trying to kill her. How could she expect him to?

When Cody reached for the door handle, a soft sob stopped him. His daughter, probably confused by Bethany's mad dash out the door, began to cry. Mrs. Snow, who'd been frozen in place, suddenly scrambled around the kitchen. "Where's the phone? Where's the phone!" she exclaimed, and her hand shook as she shoved baking sheets and cookie tins aside in search of it.

Cody pulled out his cell and handed it to her. "Call the sheriff, and keep an eye on Molly," he said. Then he leaned down and kissed his daughter's cheek. "I'll make sure Bethany is okay," he told her. "I'll make sure nothing happens to her."

He wasn't sure how he was going to do that. He didn't have a gun like she did. He didn't even have any idea what she'd seen out the window. He hadn't been able to focus on anything but her in that moment, when she'd been more worried that she was putting him and Molly in danger than she was worried about herself.

That was why she'd stayed away from him since the crash, not because she'd suspected him of being responsible. But because she'd worried that *she* was...

Just because she'd been doing her job.

"Daddy!" Molly called out when he opened the door. "She told you to stay here."

And clearly Molly, with tears streaking down her face, wanted him to stay. But he couldn't stand by and wait for help to arrive while Bethany rushed off to confront a threat on her own. He had to help.

Somehow...

"I'll be right back," he said. As he stepped out and shut the door, he heard Mrs. Snow calling out to him.

"Cody—"

He didn't need her to tell him what he already knew. That he was acting rashly. At the moment, it was all he could do. Because he couldn't do what Bethany wanted him to do: nothing at all. He had to protect her, but first he had to find her.

Once he was outside, he had no idea where she'd gone. The Snows' van was still in the driveway, his truck parked next to it. So she hadn't taken a vehicle. She'd left on foot. And when he looked down at the driveway, he noticed her prints in the fluffy snow that was falling so heavily. She hadn't headed toward the street, which was what she'd been staring at out the bay window in the living room.

She'd obviously seen something or someone out there. So why hadn't she headed that way? He tracked her through the backyard then through the neighbor's yard next door. Dogs barked as he approached the fence of the next yard. Had she hopped over that?

Had she continued on this way? He looked around, but the grass was warmer than the asphalt, so the snow was already beginning to melt on it. The ground hadn't frozen yet; he should have been relieved. He would be able to resume construction of the new barn. But he didn't care about his plans for the ranch right now.

He cared about Bethany and making sure nothing happened to her.

The barking grew louder, and there was banging against the fence as the dogs hurled themselves against it. Surely Bethany wouldn't have risked going through that yard.

He wouldn't. So he slipped along the outside of the fence, through the side yards until he came out onto the street. Kids were playing in a front yard a few houses down, trying to build a snowman even though the light snow wouldn't pack. Giving up, they flung loose snow-balls at each other that fell apart before reaching their targets.

Bethany hadn't rushed for her gun to stop a snowball fight. She was nowhere near them. So where was she? And how had she disappeared so quickly?

Because she was a professional. He had to remind himself she'd had years of experience at her job. But the only memory that stuck in his head at the moment was of finding that SUV in the ditch with her slumped over the wheel, unconscious.

It could have been worse; he could have found her

dead. For a few terrifying seconds, he'd thought she was. Hadn't it been an accident? Was someone actually trying to kill her? If so, her rushing out to confront them was only going to make it easier for them.

Ignoring the kids, Cody focused on the street. That was where Bethany had been staring. What had drawn her attention? Some vehicles were parked at the curb, snow accumulating on their roofs and hoods—except for one. Except for a truck that the snow melted off because it was running, its exhaust rising like a cloud behind it. And the front of it…had only one headlamp.

Cody remembered the glass in the road at the crash site that he'd crunched under his tires and his boots. Was it the vehicle that had rear ended the SUV Bethany had been driving? And if it had just been an accident, what was it doing here? Parked far enough away from the Snow house not to be noticed but close enough to watch it?

His heart beat faster as he realized that Bethany was right. Someone had followed her here and, since they'd forced her off the road, they obviously wanted to hurt her.

Where was she?

Was he already too late?

But then the truck wouldn't be there still, idling at the curb.

Obviously the driver hadn't seen her yet either, or they would have pulled away. But then the truck did edge away from the curb. He suspected that the driver had seen him, standing in that front yard, gaping at the street. Because the vehicle headed in his direction.

He glanced toward the kids, worried that the truck might jump the curb and strike them. But they'd disappeared. So he had only himself to worry about, but he was frozen in place, unsure of where to move, where to run...

The vehicle didn't head toward the sidewalk, instead the window just lowered. He couldn't see the driver—just the barrel of a gun as it fired at him.

Bethany couldn't stop shaking. It had all happened so quickly. Seeing the truck. Rushing out with her gun. Seeing those kids playing so close to that truck. She hadn't wanted to risk confronting the driver and having those kids get hurt. Just like she hadn't wanted Cody to get hurt either.

She'd told him to stay inside, to protect his daughter and her mom.

Instead he'd risked his life.

He would have lost it if she hadn't been there, if she hadn't knocked him to the ground just as that shot rang out. She wasn't sure even now if he was okay or if he'd been hit. He hadn't moved since she'd knocked him down. She hadn't either. She lay sprawled across him.

He suddenly gasped and gulped in a mouthful of air before his hands clutched her, running over her back. "Are you okay?" he asked.

"No!" she exclaimed. After a glance at the street to make sure the truck was gone, she finally jumped up. Her legs were shaking so badly they nearly folded beneath her. She was furious with him for not listening to her.

He scrambled up and grasped her shoulders. Staring

down into her face, his green eyes full of concern and fear, he asked, "Were you hit?"

"No!" she exclaimed. "But you could have been! Were you?" She ran her gaze over him, checking for blood. But his jeans were just damp from the wet snow. His hair damp and mussed, too.

"I'm fine," he said, then he glanced around. "Where did the kids go?"

"I got them into their house," she said. Just in time. She peered at all the houses, checking for broken glass, broken windows. The driver had barely lowered their window, so the barrel hadn't been pointing directly out. It had fired more into the air than at a target. But still the bullet could have landed somewhere.

She shivered.

"You're cold," Cody said. "We should go into the house."

She shook her head as sirens whined in the distance. "I'm not cold." Anger heated her flesh as it coursed through her. If she went inside, she couldn't yell at him like she wanted to, like she had to. "What were you thinking? I told you to stay inside the house, to stay with Mom and Molly!" Emotion choked her over how close she could have come to losing him. No. She'd lost him long ago. But... "Molly," she said. "Why weren't you thinking about her? You're all she has! She can't lose you!"

Cody started shaking then, and all the color drained from his face. "You're right. I don't know what I was thinking."

She wasn't sure what she'd been thinking either. She should have made sure he wouldn't follow her, or her mother or Molly. She shouldn't have run off before backup arrived. But she hadn't liked that truck being so close to the house, to people she cared so much about… and she'd wanted to make sure the person inside didn't try anything.

Like shooting at them. Like they had.

"Did you see the driver?" she asked.

He shook his head. "Just the gun…" He shivered again, and she worried that he was probably freezing in his damp clothes.

"Go inside," she told him as her father's SUV pulled across the end of the driveway.

"I'm sorry," Cody said. "I'm sorry I got in the way and he got away. I'm sorry." He grimaced.

"Go inside," she told him. "Make sure your daughter is all right."

"Oh, no… I hope she didn't hear the gunshot."

There was no way that she hadn't since the sound of it was ringing yet in Bethany's ears. It had been close, much too close, and loud. Whoever was home in the area, and for miles around, had to have heard it and now the sirens.

Cody must have realized that, too, because he turned to head toward her house, but then he stopped and froze. And she worried that he had been hurt and maybe just hadn't noticed his wound yet because of the shock.

"Cody!" she called out to him. "Are you all right?"

Then she glanced behind him and saw Molly standing there with her mother. Both of them appeared to be shaking like she'd been. Bethany was calmer now.

The truck wouldn't return now for another drive-by, not with the police presence. Not only had her father arrived in his SUV with lights flashing and sirens blaring but a couple of state troopers had pulled onto the street as well. They were safe, which was probably why her mother had come outside with Molly. Otherwise, she knew Sally Snow would never put a child in danger.

But Bethany felt like she herself had. While they were safe right now, she wasn't sure how long they would be when whoever was after her was bold enough to make an attempt in front of witnesses.

It was only after Cody had walked over to his daughter and her mother that it occurred to her that the gun barrel hadn't been directed at her. She'd been careful to stay out of sight in order to not scare the driver away before she got a look at the truck. And had, hopefully, been able to sneak up on the driver and apprehend them. That shot couldn't have been meant for her. The truck had stopped at the curb in front of Cody, had pointed the gun at him.

Was someone trying to kill Cody Shepard?

If so, why?

The driver was shaking with fury and with regret.

That had been sloppy and stupid. What if someone had gotten a good look? The windows were tinted and had been steamed up from all the hours spent in it watching the house, waiting for her to leave. But she hadn't left…

Cody Shepard had. And he'd stood there, staring at the vehicle. Had he recognized it? Did he have any idea?

It couldn't be traced back directly. But Cody might

be able to track it back indirectly. To figure out who'd borrowed it and why.

Now Cody was as big a threat as Bethany Snow was.

Maybe bigger…

Now there were two threats that needed to be eliminated.

Chapter Eleven

The minute Cody crossed the yard to his daughter, he lifted her into his arms and held on as tightly as he could without hurting her. He never wanted to let her go, never wanted to risk her going on without him. Never wanted to risk losing her...like she could have just lost him if not for Bethany Snow saving his life. What had he been thinking?

He hadn't been. That was the problem. Once he had his daughter in his arms, Mrs. Snow rushed off to hug hers. But as she passed him, she patted his shoulder and whispered something through her tears. "Thank God." He had certainly helped Cody and Bethany and those innocent children avoid getting hurt. Him and Bethany. Cody uttered his own silent prayer of thanks to the Lord as he continued to hug his daughter against his madly pounding heart.

But Molly pushed against his shoulder and pulled far enough away to stare into his face. Hers was red and swollen with tears. He felt a sharp pain of regret for causing her such fear and worry. She was just a baby although if he said as much, she would argue with him. She always fought so hard to be independent, like Bethany had.

Bethany hadn't wanted to be like anyone else, hadn't wanted to settle, hadn't wanted to stay in a small town.

Someday he would probably lose Molly like he had Bethany, to bigger things. But for now, he intended to hold her close for as long as he could. "I'm sorry, sweetheart," he said. "I didn't mean to scare you."

"You didn't," she said. "The gunshot did. Did Miss Bethany shoot at you?"

"No," he assured her. "Miss Bethany didn't shoot her gun." She'd been too busy saving his life. Had he thanked her? He'd been so stunned that he didn't know if he had. She'd knocked him to the ground so hard that she'd knocked the breath out of his lungs.

"Then it must have been a hunter," Molly said. Whenever she'd heard guns go off before, it had been a hunter shooting somewhere on the ranch. "What were they shooting at?"

That had not been a hunter who'd fired that gun, at least not a hunter of animals. This person had been hunting a person.

Bethany?

Fear for her gripped him. He couldn't imagine having someone after him like whoever was after her, so determined that they'd followed her back to her hometown for the holidays. Out of vengeance? Obsession?

"There are no deer around here," Molly said as she stared around the yard. "So what would they shoot at?"

He wasn't about to admit that the gun had been pointed

at him. Then he sucked in a breath with his sudden realization, and fear for himself slammed through him.

Bethany hadn't been anywhere in sight when that
truck had rolled up to the curb, when that window had
lowered…when the gun barrel had pointed out. At *him*.

Bethany hadn't been the target. At that moment, he
had been the target.

What in the world was going on?

Did it have something to do with what he'd uncovered at the ranch? Or was it because whoever was after
Bethany wanted him out of the way?

"Did you already interview Cody?" her dad, in total
sheriff mode, asked Bethany, and his gaze moved from
her to where Cody stood in the yard with his daughter.
He didn't have a coat on, but at least her mom must have
put Molly's on her before coming outside once the police had arrived.

Her mom, thankfully, had gone back inside the house
after Bethany confessed to seeing the truck from the
crash and to all the threats she'd received. Sally was
angry that her husband and her daughter hadn't shared
everything with her before now. A twinge of guilt
struck Bethany that they hadn't. But neither of them
had wanted to upset her. She already worried too much
about Bethany as it was.

She'd been so happy that Bethany had finally come
home for the holidays, which was her mom's favorite
time of the year. Bethany hadn't wanted to ruin her
mother's enjoyment with talk of those threats. Now she
wondered, why would Jimmy Lee Howard take a shot
at Cody? How could he know what Cody had once

meant to Bethany—what he could mean again if she wasn't leaving?

His life was here now, while she'd vowed to never stay here and settle for a life like her mom's—one that was spent taking care of other people instead of herself. Cody was like her mom now. He'd given up the rodeo career he'd always dreamed of to take care of his daughter and his dad and the ranch. But he didn't seem to resent his responsibilities like she'd worried she would. He seemed to embrace and enjoy them.

Why would someone try to take a shot at Cody? A man who was as special as her mother had tried earlier to get her to admit? Would his ex have any reason to seek revenge? Maybe she hadn't willingly given up her daughter. Maybe she'd had another reason for walking away from them both.

"I need to ask him more questions," Bethany admitted to her dad. "But he was pretty shaken up right after it happened. And it happened so fast I doubt he saw anything."

"Did you see anything beyond what you already told me?" her dad asked.

She'd seen that barrel stick out the window, pointing toward Cody, if just a bit too high to actually hit him. Had it just been a warning shot? Or had the driver been making sure that nobody could see their face, could recognize them?

Was it someone Cody knew?

If so, it couldn't have been Jimmy Lee Howard.

After she'd knocked Cody to the ground, she had had the instinct to look toward the street, to watch the vehicle to make sure that it left and didn't stop so the driver could get out and fire at them some more. As it had sped off, she'd caught a couple of numbers on the license plate. She'd told her dad, who'd ordered a BOLO, be on the lookout, for an older model black Ford Super Duty truck with a broken headlamp and a Montana plate ending in 203.

"I don't remember anything else," she said. "But let me check with Cody before he and Molly leave." Earlier she'd been trying to get him to take his daughter and go home, but now that he probably intended to do exactly that, she was scared. Scared that he was in danger and she might not be able to protect him.

"I better check on your mom again," her father said, his voice gruff with emotion. "I can't stand it when she's upset with me."

Her brow furrowed at his admission. She never remembered it bothering him before, when he'd missed all those school events and church socials and his wife had expressed her disappointment over his not making time for them. He'd shrugged off her complaints then, but maybe he hadn't realized yet that his wife had been parenting alone even when he wasn't deployed.

While he walked down the drive toward the house, Bethany headed back to where Cody and his daughter stood yet in the neighbor's front yard. Cody's back was to her, and the two were engrossed in conversation so neither of them noticed her walking up, allowing her to blatantly eavesdrop.

"You should buy Miss Bethany a real big Christmas present so that she stops being mad at you," Molly suggested.

Bethany felt a pang of regret that Molly must have overheard her yelling at Cody.

"I don't know what she wants," Cody replied to his daughter. Then beneath his breath, he added, "I never did…"

"Maybe she can tell Santa."

"You need to go see Santa," Cody said. "You need to tell him—and me—what you want for Christmas."

Molly giggled and shook her head. "Just Santa. Maybe Miss Bethany can come with us to see him, and she can talk to him, too."

Cody released a weary-sounding sigh. "Don't get your hopes up that she'll join us, Molly," he said. "She's really busy and might not have time for us."

Molly uttered her own weary-sounding sigh then and laid her head against Cody's shoulder. "Like Mommy."

And Bethany's heart cracked with the pain she heard in the little girl's voice. While Molly always seemed so bright and happy, it was clear she missed her mother. The little girl could not lose her father, too. Bethany had to find out who'd fired that shot. She had to make sure Cody didn't get hurt or worse.

She had to make sure she didn't inadvertently hurt him or his daughter either. Hating to intrude on their moment, Bethany took a step back, planning to turn for home, but the movement must have caught Molly's attention because she raised her head from her dad's shoulder. "Miss Bethany." She sounded tired and shy.

Bethany regretted how harshly she'd spoken to Cody in front of his daughter. The little girl was too young to understand that Bethany had only been trying to protect him. She offered the child a reassuring smile. "Hey, Molly," she said. "I'm very sorry about earlier."

"Daddy said you didn't shoot him," Molly said.

Bethany gasped that the little girl would actually think that. But she had seen Bethany with a gun earlier, so she hadn't jumped that far to her conclusion. Not as far as Bethany had jumped when she'd considered that the body Cody had found might have belonged to Molly's mother.

"I would never shoot your daddy," she promised.

"You were really mad at him," Molly said.

"That's what I'm sorry about," Bethany said. "I shouldn't have yelled like I did. I just didn't want him to get hurt."

"Me neither," Molly agreed.

"Me neither." Cody gave a slightly shaky chuckle.

Bethany suspected he'd realized what she had—that that gun had been pointed at him. "I can't imagine why anyone would want to," she continued, and then she met Cody's gaze and held it. "Can you?"

With no hesitation he shook his head. "Nobody."

"It must have been a hunter then," Molly said with a child's simple logic. And in her mind, hopefully, it was settled, so she wouldn't worry about her dad.

Bethany was worried enough for the both of them. "Yup, must have been…" But who had they been hunting, Bethany or Cody?

Molly wriggled down from her father's arms. "I better go back and help Mrs. Snow with the cookies. She has a lot of them left to decorate."

"No, sweetheart, we should really go now," Cody said. "It's getting late." And he looked exhausted.

"I'm sure my mom has a few cookies ready for her to take home," Bethany said. "Let Molly get those and your coat for you."

As if just realizing that he wasn't wearing his coat, Cody rubbed the sleeves of his flannel shirt. "I can—"

"Wait." Bethany caught his arm and held him back from following his daughter as the little girl scampered across the yard toward the two-story colonial.

"Want to yell at me some more when she can't hear?" he asked with a tired smile.

She shook her head. "I am sorry about that…"

He sighed, and it sounded ragged. "No. I'm sorry. I shouldn't have followed you out. I screwed up. And I owe you. You saved my life."

She shook her head again. "I doubt you would have been hit…" This time. But what if the shooter came after him again?

He shuddered, probably more with fear than cold. "I'm glad I didn't have to find out," he said. "I'm glad you were there."

"Me, too." She nodded.

"I don't know how you do it," he said. "How you put your life at risk like you do."

She sighed. Here it was, the criticism she'd heard from the few guys she'd dated over the years who hadn't liked her career, who hadn't respected her choices.

"You're incredibly brave," he said. "But then you always were. I'm glad you got everything you always wanted."

She waited for the flood of pride at his unexpected praise. She had worked hard. She did take risks. But instead of being pleased that he admired her, she felt a flash of disappointment. Because this past week in Bear Creek had her wondering if she *did* have everything she wanted.

There was nothing for her here career-wise, but she wanted to make sure that there was something else here. That Cody and Molly and her family stayed safe and happy. It wasn't until later that night, long after Cody and Molly had left, that Bethany finally got some answers.

Her phone rang with a call from her bureau chief in Chicago. "Sorry, Snow, I don't want to keep disturbing you on vacation—"

"It's fine," she assured him. It was hardly a vacation now. "Did you find Jimmy Lee Howard?"

"Yup," he said.

"Is he here? Did he follow me to Montana?"

He chuckled. "Nope. He's been in the hospital. Tried abducting the wrong woman in a gym parking lot. She fractured his jaw and broke his arm. And his other arm has been handcuffed to his hospital bed since it happened. He hasn't been anywhere near you."

"But the break-in…"

The chief sighed. "Some kids got busted in your neighborhood breaking into houses looking for prescription drugs and alcohol."

She huffed. "Well, they were disappointed with my place." She hadn't either for them to take.

He chuckled. "You okay?"

"No," she admitted. "I thought for sure it was Jimmy Lee…" And now that she knew it wasn't, she had to look closer at everyone in Bear Creek.

After she ended the call with her boss, her cell vibrated

again in her hand. Had he forgotten something? Or maybe he was just going to ask if she'd made a decision yet on that promotion.

But then she saw that it wasn't a call but a voice mail reminder from an earlier call she'd missed—when she'd been trying to catch the driver of that truck, when she'd been saving Cody from a bullet. She clicked on the voice mail for it to play.

"Agent Snow, this is Marcy Cruise from the state police lab. You wanted a rush on those DNA results you submitted earlier this week. We were able to confirm a familial match between the sample you sent and the remains found the week before. The victim was the mother."

She sucked in a breath of shock that it was Cody's mother. But maybe she shouldn't have been surprised it was Kim Shepard. The details of her leaving had always been more gossip than fact. How would Cody feel about it? Would he be relieved that his mother hadn't left him by choice? That she'd been taken away from him?

Was the murderer now trying to take Cody away from his daughter? Her pulse quickened with fear over Molly losing her father, over her own loss if something happened to Cody. Not that they'd had anything to do with each other the past dozen years...

She considered calling him with the news and with a warning. But it was late. And he'd already looked exhausted when he and Molly had left for the ranch. She'd told him then to be careful, and he'd given her a solemn nod and the promise that he would.

"Please, God, help him keep that promise," she murmured, relying on her faith like her mother had taught her. For so long she'd struggled with it, after all the evil she'd seen, but now she turned toward it, embracing it. "Please, God, keep Cody Shepard and his little girl safe."

Then Bethany could concentrate on finding a killer… before they killed again.

Chapter Twelve

Cody had been exhausted by the time he and Molly headed back to the ranch, but as tired as he'd been, he hadn't gotten any sleep. And it hadn't been because of nearly getting shot. He hadn't even had the chance to think about that.

Thanks to Snowball.

The little ball of white fluff had been sick the entire night, and Cody was worried. His daughter loved her kitty so much she couldn't lose her, not after coming uncomfortably close to losing her father. Hopefully she didn't know how close it had been, that someone had purposely pointed a gun in his direction.

Maybe the bullet wouldn't have hit him, but he was glad that Bethany Snow had made certain he hadn't had to find out. She'd saved him.

He was counting on a different woman to save Snowball—his former stepmom, Roberta. Molly had insisted on coming along, which he'd worried wasn't a good idea, in case something was seriously wrong with her kitty and Roberta couldn't save it. But he hadn't had the heart to separate them, and he knew Molly would have been distraught the entire time he and Snowball were at the veterinarian clinic if he'd left her home with Sammy.

"You really think Miss Roberta can fix Snowball?" she asked as he pulled into the parking lot of the big barn that Roberta had converted into her practice years before she'd married his father. The woman was Bethany's idol because she'd done all this on her own, completing college and veterinarian school and establishing her practice. She hadn't needed anyone.

Cody's father had needed her and still needed her. Cody wasn't sure why they'd split; it had happened while he'd been traveling the rodeo circuit. If he and Roberta had been closer, he might have asked her why she'd filed, but even before his Alzheimer's diagnosis, his father had never talked about anything but the ranch and the cattle. So maybe Roberta had just gotten bored like Cody's mother had. But why hadn't his mother taken him along with her when she'd left? Had she known then what he hadn't even realized until recently? That he loved the ranch, too.

While he'd enjoyed traveling with the rodeo during those years he'd chased his teenage dreams, Cody had always had a hollow ache inside him, as if something was missing. Back then he'd thought it was Bethany, and he'd tried replacing her with Theresa. She'd reminded him of Bethany because she was strong and independent. But unlike Bethany, she'd had the same interests he had—they'd shared their love of the rodeo.

Cody was the one who'd changed. After they'd had Molly, and their little girl had gotten closer to school age, he'd no longer wanted to travel. But Theresa had chosen to give up them rather than the rodeo. After admitting she had no interest in being a wife and mother, she'd taken to traveling separately from them even before the divorce. To his surprise, Cody had no qualms about giving up the rodeo to bring his daughter home to the ranch. For the first time in a long time, he'd felt at home. Molly loved it here, too, loved the small town and making friends and going to church and preschool.

And her kitty...

He parked the truck next to the front door of Roberta's clinic, and Molly, who was holding the listless Snowball, struggled to free herself from her booster seat with one hand. Cody jumped out of the truck and hurried around to her side to help her and her precious cargo onto the asphalt. Then he hurried toward the door. It was locked but rattled as someone unlocked and opened it. With dark circles beneath her dark eyes and her brown hair clipped back in a messy ponytail, Roberta looked as if she hadn't gotten much more sleep than he had.

"I'm sorry it's so early," Cody said. "Thanks for opening before your usual hours for us."

Roberta shook her head. "It's no problem. You should have called me last night. I was out on some calls anyway and would have stopped at the ranch."

"I told you to call last night," Molly managed through the tears choking her.

"I thought she ate something off the Christmas tree. And that it would pass and she'd feel better," Cody said.

"It might be the tree itself that made her sick," Roberta remarked. "Is it a pine?"

Cody nodded. "Yes..."

"The sap or the water in the basin can make cats very sick."

Molly gasped and began to cry. Cody picked up both his daughter and the pet, cradling them in his arms. "Can you please help her?" Cody asked, his heart breaking along with his daughter's.

"I'll do my very best," Roberta assured them. Then she escorted them through the reception area into one of the small exam rooms. Once inside, she gently plucked the lethargic kitty from Molly's arms. "You told me she was throwing up, so she might have already cleared the toxins. But I'll give her some charcoal to absorb the last of it."

"And she'll be okay?" Molly asked.

Roberta was listening to the kitty's heart and lungs and nodded. "I think she'll be fine. Why don't you help me treat her?"

Molly wriggled down from Cody's arms to tentatively approach the woman who should have been her grandmother. Too bad Roberta had divorced his dad before Molly was born and she didn't come around the ranch anymore. The veterinarian was patient and sweet with his little girl, teaching her how to treat her kitty, and Molly hung on her every word.

She was so compassionate. After Snowball threw up again, she helped Roberta clean her up and then cradled her in her arms, singing softly to her. He and his former stepmother left the two of them in the exam room and backed out into the reception area.

"I think she'll be fine," Roberta assured him.

"The cat or my kid?" he asked with a shaky breath.

"Both of them," she said. "Just keep the cat away from the tree. It'll be a little harder to protect your daughter."

He nodded. "The world is a scary place."

"Yes," Roberta said. "I hear you had a scare yesterday at the Snow place."

Cody shuddered in remembrance. "Gotta love small towns, huh?"

She chuckled. "You know how gossip spreads around Bear Creek."

"I figured you were always too busy to listen to it," he said. She'd always seemed above all that, totally focused on her practice.

She shrugged. "I usually am, except when it concerns you or your dad. I worry about you, Cody." Her forehead creased with concern. "You have so much on your plate, with what you found at the ranch and your father, and now somebody was shooting at you?"

He shook his head. "I don't know if that had anything to do with me…" He wasn't sure how it could have. "It's not like I know anything about that body."

"Was it her daddy then?" Roberta asked with a chuckle. "Firing a warning shot because you're seeing Bethany Snow again?"

"I'm not seeing Bethany," Cody said. "She has no interest in me beyond what was found out at the ranch. She's only home for the holidays and then she wants to leave Bear Creek just as badly as she ever did."

Roberta nodded. "She always had big dreams."

"You inspired her," Cody said. Roberta Kline had been a positive role model for Bethany. Maybe she could be the same for his little girl since Bethany wasn't going to stick around…

"Bethany definitely went on to achieve all those big dreams she had as a teenager," Roberta said.

Cody nodded. "Yes, she did."

"She's a lot more successful in law enforcement than her daddy ever was," Roberta said. "It's no wonder Sheriff Snow enlisted her to help."

"Cold cases are her specialty," Cody said. Or so all the news reports had claimed when she'd caught that serial killer and closed so many cold cases. "She also has more experience investigating murders than he does."

"It was for sure a murder?" Roberta asked.

Cody tensed for a moment, wondering if he'd revealed too much. But this was Roberta; he trusted her. "Looked like it, body found in a barrel like it was." He cringed at the reminder of what the excavator had uncovered.

Roberta grimaced. "Well, it must've been dumped there by someone passing through. Nobody in Bear Creek would do something like that...or shoot at you for that matter."

"No," Cody agreed. "Bethany suspects that someone followed her home from Chicago. Some psychotic fan of that serial killer she caught. That's probably who forced her off the road the other night and fired those shots."

Roberta released a shaky breath and then shook her head. "Guess it's good you're not seeing her then, Cody. You wouldn't want to get caught in the cross fire." Her brows drew together. "Or, God forbid, have your daughter caught in it."

Panic gripped his heart at the thought of what could have happened if Molly had followed him out like he'd followed Bethany out. "That's the last thing I want.

Bethany Snow is the last thing that Molly or I need in our lives." Because she would only break his heart again and his daughter's, too, this time when she left. He had to stay away from her.

But Roberta's eyes widened with surprise as she stared over his shoulder. He turned to find Bethany standing inside the front door, which Roberta must have left unlocked. He felt a pang of regret Bethany had overheard what he'd said, but maybe it was for the best. She wouldn't have to worry about hurting his feelings like she had last time.

Even though she'd dumped him, she'd cried even harder than he had because she'd felt so badly for going after what she wanted. Because he hadn't wanted to get in her way while she followed her dreams, he'd kept his ring in his pocket. He wasn't about to dig it out of the drawer where he kept it now, not when he knew she was leaving soon.

Bethany sucked in a breath at the sharpness of Cody's words. He didn't look embarrassed or regretful that she'd overheard. Roberta was the one whose face flushed with embarrassment, probably over the situation she was in—once again in the middle of them.

Bethany shouldn't have been surprised Cody wanted nothing to do with her, not after how she'd treated him all those years ago. How she'd told him that it had only been puppy love and not real.

If that had been the case, why had she missed him for so long?

Why—even now—did she still have this hollow ache inside her?

Like something was missing no matter how much success she'd achieved, how many promotions she was offered, how many cases she closed. But she would be a fool to turn down the promotion she'd been offered. To live and work in New York, to run her own team—it was all she'd thought she'd wanted. She would be so busy, busier than her father had ever been, so she knew she would have no time for a personal life. No time to think about Cody Shepard and his little girl.

Roberta cleared her throat and greeted her, "Hello, Bethany…"

"Bethany! Miss Bethany!" a little voice called out and Molly scrambled out of a door and rushed up to greet her. A sleeping kitty was clutched close against her chest. "Did you come to check on Snowball?"

"I didn't know Snowball was sick," she said. Sammy Felton hadn't shared that when he'd said Cody and his daughter had gone to see the vet. She'd figured he was just visiting, and she'd thought it might be the perfect place to tell him about his mother, with Roberta there to offer her support. But now she wondered if that was appropriate. It would be best to talk to him alone when his daughter wasn't present. She was still processing what she'd overheard, and she needed to collect herself before figuring out how to tell him about his mother.

"Are you bringing an animal to the vet?" Molly asked, and she peered around her as if looking for Bethany's pet.

Bethany shook her head. "No. I don't have any."

"No dog or cat?" Molly asked, and it was clear Bethany had disappointed her.

She shook her head. "My landlord doesn't allow them."

And it wasn't as if she'd have the time for one even if Mr. Reynolds had agreed to let her have a pet.

"Maybe at your new place they'll let you keep one," Cody suggested.

She shrugged. She hadn't even looked for a new place yet. She hadn't even decided if she was going to accept the promotion and move to New York. Turning it down was certain to affect her career, but accepting would guarantee all she would have *was* her career. She wouldn't have time for anything else, and she wouldn't do to anyone what her father had done to his family— been too busy to be there for them.

She drew in a shaky breath. "Is Snowball going to be all right?" she asked.

Molly turned toward Roberta, who nodded. "Yes, I think she'll just be tired for a bit but once she eats, she should bounce back."

"What happened?" Bethany asked with genuine concern. She hadn't had to spend much time around Molly to know how important her kitty was to her.

"She ate the Christmas tree," Molly replied.

"The water or the sap is probably what she got into," Roberta explained.

Cody sighed, and now he looked regretful. "I should have gotten a fake one. I just thought for Molly's first Christmas at the ranch that a real one, with the smell and the…"

"Mess," Roberta teased. "The fake one will be much safer for the cat. But make sure not to use tinsel. That can cause stomach issues for inquisitive kittens, too."

Cody nodded. "After we bring Snowball home, we'll go

into town later tonight and get a fake tree to replace that one. We can see Santa then, too."

"Will you help us decorate the fake one like you did the real one?" Molly asked Bethany.

She hesitated long enough to give Cody a chance to object. He'd just said he didn't want her in his or his daughter's life. But maybe, knowing she'd overheard, he expected her to make her excuses. She smiled for Molly and told her, "I have to bring something to my dad at his work, but I can meet you in town later." That might be easier to get a chance to talk to Cody alone if she could enlist her mom to watch Molly.

"You can talk to Santa with me!" Molly exclaimed with excitement.

Bethany smiled. "Well, maybe not *with* you. But I can meet you in town square."

"You don't have to do that," Cody said, "if you're busy."

"There's something I need to talk to you about," she admitted. If she waited until after she stopped by the sheriff's office, she might have even more to share with him. Like Sammy Felton's real identity...

Since she hadn't found much of a trace of the man, she'd wanted to get a fingerprint from him. So when she'd walked away, she'd "accidentally" dropped her sunglasses onto the porch. When he'd picked them up, he'd handed them back to her with a nice thumbprint on one of the lenses. She would have brought them straight to the sheriff's office to run the print, but Roberta's practice was on the way, so she'd stopped.

She should have known this wouldn't be a good time to tell Cody about his mother. Would there ever be a good time? If he was the family of any other murder victim, she wouldn't have hesitated to inform him about what had happened to his mother. What had really happened to her...

But this was Cody.

Even though he'd always acted as if his mother's desertion hadn't bothered him, Bethany had known him well enough to know it had. She'd seen how he'd longed for a mom like hers, one that had been so nurturing and loving. Sally Snow would have never abandoned her family.

But neither had Kim Shepard, and it was past time everyone learned that.

Roberta cleared her throat again, and Bethany realized she'd been standing there without saying anything else. Cody hadn't asked why she wanted to talk to him, but maybe his former stepmother was wondering; obviously she didn't think it was a good idea for Cody to get involved with her again. She must still care about him a great deal and didn't want him getting hurt when Bethany left.

"I'll see you later," Bethany said, but she spoke to Molly and, unable to help herself, she leaned down and pressed a kiss to the little girl's forehead.

"You should kiss Snowball, too," Molly said. "It might make her feel better."

So Bethany obligingly kissed the top of the kitten's head.

Molly nodded in approval. "We better bring Snowball back to the ranch, Daddy. She's very sleepy." The lids over Molly's green eyes looked heavy, too, as if she was struggling to keep them up. And there were dark circles beneath Cody's eyes.

Had they been awake all night with the cat or because they'd been worried about that gunshot at her parents' house? Bethany needed to make sure they weren't put in danger again; she had to keep them safe.

"Thanks again, Roberta, for opening up early for us," Cody told his former stepmother, but he didn't kiss her cheek nor did the woman offer it. While they'd once been related, they'd only seemed to really talk to each other when Cody had come by the practice when Bethany had been working. He nodded at Bethany before lifting up his daughter and her cat and carrying them out to his truck.

When the door closed behind them, Bethany uttered a sigh, and Roberta echoed it. "Poor Cody," the older woman murmured. "He has his hands full and then some."

"Yes, he does," Bethany said. And he was about to get more dumped on his plate when she told him whose body he'd dug up on the ranch.

"Your mama helps him a lot," Roberta said. "But then your mama helps everybody…"

"Yes, she does," Bethany agreed.

Roberta chuckled. "Guess that's her career, huh? She's not like you and me."

"No." That would have made Bethany happy once, that she was nothing like her mother, but now she felt a flash of regret she wasn't more like Sally Snow, more compassionate and loving. Unselfish.

"Is that a good thing?" Bethany wondered aloud.

"You used to think so," Roberta reminded her. "You never wanted to rely on a man and a family to make you happy. You wanted to fulfill yourself with your education, with your career…"

"I did," Bethany agreed. "I do. But you don't think it's possible to have it all?"

"I tried," Roberta said and sighed again.

"I hate to pry," Bethany said. "But is that why your marriage to Don Shepard ended? Because you were too busy?"

"Are you asking out of personal curiosity or is this a professional inquiry?" Roberta asked, but she was smiling, as if it really didn't matter.

Bethany chuckled. "I've looked up to you a long time, Roberta," Bethany reminded her, "and if you couldn't do it, I don't have a chance."

Roberta tilted her head and studied her face. "Are you wondering about this now for any particular reason… like Cody? Or did you leave someone back in Chicago that you care about?"

She'd left nothing back in Chicago. And the realization was sobering. She had some friends, but just through work. That was the only thing she really had in common with any of them. Bethany shrugged. "I've been too busy to even think about a relationship," she admitted. But as busy as she'd been, she'd still found the time to think about Cody over the years.

"It wasn't being busy that ended my relationship," Roberta said. "I truly think *I* could have made it work. But it takes two."

"Don was too busy with the ranch?" Bethany asked. He'd been a lot like her father, with work consuming his life, leaving little time for anything else. That was probably why everyone had assumed Kim had left him, because he hadn't made time for her.

Roberta grimaced, making the lines in her face more

pronounced, making her look older. "It wasn't just the ranch. He was so bitter, and after Cody left—" she shuddered "—it got worse."

Alarm shot through Bethany. "Was he violent? Did he hurt you?"

Roberta shook her head as if shaking off bad memories. "It doesn't matter. He isn't that man anymore. With the way his mind is failing…"

"His mind," Bethany said. "Not his body." She'd only seen him briefly, and while he'd looked older, he'd gotten around easily enough. "Do you think he would have ever hurt—"

"His first wife?" Roberta asked. She shrugged. "I figured she left him because he hadn't made time for her and she'd found someone who made her a priority."

But Kim Shepard hadn't left. Bethany wasn't about to share that news with anyone else before she told Cody, though.

"Cody," Bethany said. "Back in school, he'd have bruises on him from time to time or favor his ribs. He always claimed it was because he'd been practicing for the rodeo. That he got bucked off a bronco or a bull…"

Roberta nodded. "That's probably what happened. But I do know that Don didn't approve of Cody joining the rodeo. He didn't want his son to follow in the footsteps of his philandering younger brother."

Bethany knew that, too, but she wondered now just how vehemently Don had disapproved. Back then she'd believed Cody about his bruises, but now after all her years as an investigator, she knew people often lied about being victims of domestic violence, either out of pride or some misplaced loyalty to their abusers. She and Cody had been so close that she'd thought they'd shared everything. Was it possible that he'd been protecting his dad even then?

"But Cody's home now," Roberta said. "Taking care of the ranch and his dad, and he has that big guy helping him."

But was Sammy Felton helping or hurting? Bethany had to find out who the man really was.

A car pulled into the lot, the lights shining through the glass.

"My receptionist is here," Roberta said.

"I better go," Bethany said. "You're busy."

"You are, too, taking on this case even when you're supposed to be on vacation for the holidays," Roberta said.

"There are certain professions that rarely give you any time off," Bethany said. "We both have one of those."

Roberta nodded. "Yes, you said you were stopping by the sheriff's office. Do you have a lead?"

"I don't know what I have," Bethany admitted. She also wasn't as sure about what she wanted as she'd once been. Was it possible that as she'd gotten older, she was beginning to change like Cody had? That things that weren't important to her suddenly mattered more? Like her family, like her faith…like the thought of having a family of her own? She'd been praying more lately than she had in years, praying for Cody and Molly and even for herself, so that she could make the right decisions. So that she didn't cause anyone pain.

"Thanks for talking to me," she told Roberta.

Roberta smiled. "Anytime. I've missed you."

"Me, too," Bethany said. She headed out to the SUV

that she and her father had picked up that morning from the body shop. But she didn't get far from the veterinarian clinic before she noticed that someone was following her.

Or was she just paranoid?

There weren't many roads that headed into Bear Creek, so maybe it was just someone innocently heading the same place she was. Or maybe it was that vehicle with the broken headlamp.

She slowed down and waited for it to get closer.

Chapter Thirteen

There's something I need to talk to you about...

Ever since she'd said it, that phrase had been echoing in Cody's mind. She'd found out something he wasn't going to like about the murder. That had to be it.

There was nothing else between them. She'd heard what he'd told Roberta, so it wasn't as if she had to spell it out for him like she had all those years ago. They wanted different things out of life, and there was no way they would ever be able to build a life together.

Back then he'd been naive enough to think they could both make compromises and make a long-distance relationship work. But she'd pointed out that it was more than that; that they had nothing in common. They had even less in common now than they'd had then.

He hadn't been able to make a marriage last with a woman with whom he'd had a lot in common—careers and a child. So he had no hope with Bethany.

Not anymore.

He glanced across the truck console at his daughter. She'd fallen asleep, slumped in her booster seat, her cheek on Snowball's fur. The cat was awake but barely, just enough that her eyes were blue slits in her furry white face. But she looked better than she'd had, thanks to Roberta. The little thing was going to make it. He uttered a soft sigh, reluctant to wake Molly.

He'd pulled into the driveway moments before next to where Sammy's truck should have been parked had he been home. Where was he? It was awful early for his dad to be up, and Sammy wouldn't have left him alone in the house.

Or so Cody hoped…

Maybe Bethany's cynicism was rubbing off on Cody, or maybe after what had happened yesterday, he was getting a bit suspicious himself. But Sammy had been acting oddly since the body had been found. Or was it since Bethany had showed up?

Cody had once told him about Bethany, years ago, when they'd shared stories of women who'd broken their hearts. A few had broken Sammy's; that was why he'd sworn to remain single the rest of his life, claiming Cody and Molly were the only family he needed…since he had nobody else.

Why did he have nobody else? Because of his broken heart? Or…

Cody sighed again and shook his head. He needed to sleep, too. And he wasn't about to do that in the truck like Molly. He opened his door. But before he came around to her side, he climbed the few steps to the back door and opened it.

And he was really glad he'd left Molly asleep in the truck.

Blood pooled on the kitchen floor and spattered the

walls. Had Sammy cut himself while he was cooking? But there was nothing on the stove, counters or kitchen table.

Just the floor.

And if Sammy was the one who'd been injured, how had he driven his truck away?

He wouldn't have let Don drive; the man wouldn't have remembered how to get to town let alone to the hospital. And clearly whoever had been cut needed to go to the hospital.

"Sammy!" he shouted, his heart pounding hard and fast with fear for his friend and his father. "Dad?"

But he wasn't expecting an answer. Just in case someone was here and couldn't speak, he stepped through the kitchen doorway and went into the dining room, where he found more blood spattered on the floor and the wall and across the jagged pieces of glass sticking out of a broken mirror...

What happened?

His hand shaking, he pulled out his cell phone and pushed in the contact for Sammy. As he did, he walked back to the kitchen and jerked open the drawer where Sammy's phone had been a week ago. It was gone now. But there was blood smeared on the front of that drawer and inside it.

Were there two crime scenes on the ranch now? One at the old homestead and one inside the house? He shook at the thought.

And then a little voice tremulously queried, "Daddy, is that blood?" Molly stood inside the open kitchen doorway, Snowball clutched in her hands.

"Don't come in this way, honey," he told her. "Sammy must have spilled ketchup all over…"

"That doesn't look like ketchup," she dubiously replied. The child was too smart for four, too smart for him to fool.

Sammy's cell went to voice mail, just as Cody had worried it would. "Let's go in the front," he said, leading her out of the kitchen and along the wraparound porch to that door, which was unlocked. But doors were rarely locked in Bear Creek, where nothing bad was ever supposed to happen.

That was why Cody had brought his daughter home, to protect her from the dangers of life on the road. But there were dangers here that he'd never known.

Molly stepped inside the foyer and stared up at him, her green eyes narrowed and full of wisdom beyond her tender years. "What's going on, Daddy?"

He shrugged. "I don't know, honey. I'll find out." But before he hit redial, he helped her with her coat and boots. "Go upstairs to keep Snowball away from the tree—" and the blood and the glass "—and I'll take care of it."

But before he touched anything else in his house, he wanted to make sure that it wasn't really a crime scene. Once he'd closed Molly's bedroom door on her and her kitten, he hit redial.

"Cody—"

"Are you okay?" he asked, and some of his panic eased that his friend had been able to answer the phone.

"I'm fine, but, Cody…"

"What is it?" he asked. "What happened? Where are you?"

"Your dad cut himself pretty bad. I didn't want to wait for an ambulance, so I used my belt as a tourniquet and drove him to the hospital. We just got here now."

"I can grab Molly and meet you down there," Cody said.

"No, you guys were up all night, and you gave me that form so I can authorize medical treatment for him," Sammy reminded him. "You don't have to come down. He'll want to come home the minute they finish stitching him up anyway."

The ranch was the one thing his father seemed to recognize even more than people. That was why Cody didn't want him sent to a memory center. All his father's memories were here. And Cody wanted to keep him here with them, at the ranch, for as long as he could.

"Get some rest," Sammy said. "I'll clean up when I get back."

Sammy had been up all night, too, helping Cody clean up after the sick cat. Tears stung his eyes, gratitude overwhelming him. "What did I ever do to deserve you?" he asked, feeling a pang of guilt for letting doubts about Sammy creep up on him. Sammy had willingly given up his life with the rodeo to help Cody out with Molly and his dad at a remote ranch in Montana. He deserved Cody's loyalty, not his suspicion.

"You're a good guy, Cody," Sammy said. "One of the few true blue."

Cody chuckled at his friend's oft-repeated description of him. "You're the true blue," Cody said.

"Now," Sammy muttered.

"What?" Cody asked.

"Uh…did your lady friend find you?" Sammy asked.

"Lady friend?"

"The FBI agent," Sammy said. "She stopped by the ranch looking for you this morning."

That must have been how she'd wound up at Roberta's office. "Did she say why?" Cody asked.

"No, but your dad was pretty jacked up this morning, so I didn't have time to talk."

"What was wrong with Dad?" Cody asked. "What happened to the mirror?"

"He didn't recognize the guy in it and punched it," Sammy said. "He was staring at his own reflection."

Cody sighed and silently repeated the prayer he so often turned to in times like this, asking for help to find compassion and patience. He added one for his father to heal from his injury and find peace with the changes happening to his memory. "That's so sad…" He dealt with that sadness by turning to his faith.

"I get it," Sammy said. "Sometimes I don't recognize the guy in the mirror either."

"We all get older," Cody said.

"Says the young'un," Sammy joked. "But it's not just getting older that changes us. It's getting wiser and realizing what really matters and sometimes realizing what we've lost…"

His father had lost more than most. Two wives and now his memories.

"Are you sure I shouldn't come down there?" Cody asked. "Make sure he's okay?"

"He's okay now," Sammy said. "They gave him something to sedate him while they stitch him up. Stay there. Get some rest. We'll probably be back before you'd even make it here."

Cody breathed a sigh of relief. "Okay. Thanks, Sammy, for taking care of all of us."

"You do that, Cody. I just pitch in where I can." He disconnected the call then, as if he didn't want to hear any more of the compliments Cody wanted to lavish on him.

He really didn't know how he would have managed without his best friend. Maybe Sammy had been God's way of protecting him; the older man had taken Cody in when he'd been a rookie on the rodeo circuit, with people often commenting on their odd friendship. Sammy had always kept pretty much to himself until Cody. The only other person he'd talked to had been his uncle Shep, but he hadn't seemed to actually like Shep. But few people actually liked the womanizing narcissist. Cody understood now why his dad had been so against Cody following his uncle to join the rodeo. He probably hadn't wanted Cody to turn out like Shep.

Cody chuckled. He was the farthest thing from a womanizer, which was probably why Sammy had teased him about his *lady friend*. Whatever Bethany wanted to talk to him about had been important enough for her to track him down at Roberta's. But then she hadn't shared it with him. Because Molly and Roberta had been there?

A chill ran down his spine at the thought of what it could be. He couldn't—he wouldn't—let his mind go there. Not now.

Despite Sammy telling him not to bother, Cody busied himself cleaning up the glass and blood. It had set long enough that it wasn't easy to get out of the worn hardwood floors, so he was down on his hands and knees when a pair of leather boots entered his line of vision.

He gasped and glanced up...at Bethany. "You let yourself in the house."

"Molly did," she said. "But then she scampered back upstairs with Snowball since you hadn't gotten rid of the tree yet."

He groaned.

"She said you were busy cleaning up the ketchup that she didn't believe was really ketchup..." She peered around the kitchen and murmured, "Neither do I. What happened, Cody?"

He groaned again. "My dad cut himself. Sammy took him to town for stitches."

"Lucky he was here," she said. "This looks bad."

It had looked worse when he'd first showed up, but he wasn't about to admit that to her. He continued to gaze up at her.

"Is he going to be all right?"

He nodded. "Yes. Just some stitches."

"What happened? What did he cut himself on?"

"Why all the questions?" he asked. "This was an accident. Not a crime. There's no reason for you to investigate it. To investigate me."

"I'm not investigating *you*, Cody."

He arched a brow and studied her beautiful face. "What are you doing? Sammy said you were here this morning. That he told you I was at Roberta's, and you showed up there. Now you're back here. Are you stalking me?"

Her face flushed, and she narrowed her beautiful blue eyes in a glare. "No. I told you I wanted to talk to you."

"About what?" he asked. He waved a hand at the blood drying on the floor. "It couldn't be about this since it just happened. What's it about?"

Now the color drained from her face, leaving her ghostly pale.

And his stomach muscles tightened in apprehension. This wasn't good. "What, Bethany? Just tell me."

"It's about your mother," she said.

And he knew before she even said it. He knew.

Maybe he'd always known on some level, because the woman of his childhood memories, the woman who'd done the giggles and wiggles to get him ready to sit through church, that woman had loved him too much to leave him willingly.

"She's the body that was buried here," Bethany said gently.

He was glad he was still kneeling on the floor because if he'd been standing, his legs probably would have given out from the shock. But in some strange way, it was also a relief. Maybe he wasn't as unlovable and easy to leave as he'd thought. But then he thought of his mother, of her young life cut so cruelly short, and tears stung his eyes over her loss as much as his own. She'd lost out on so much.

Bethany stared down at Cody, unable to tell what he was feeling…if he was feeling anything at all. She'd just dropped a bombshell on him, and she wasn't sure what she expected. But nothing prepared her for how helpless he looked down there on the floor.

Cody…

She dropped to her knees in front of him and reached for his face, cupping it in her hands. His skin was so cold and pale but for those dark circles beneath his beautiful green eyes—eyes that glistened now with tears. He was hurting, and so was she—hurting for him. "Cody, are you all right?" she asked, her heart aching over his loss. It may have happened two decades ago, but now it was real. Now he knew his mother was never coming back…

That she couldn't.

"Cody?" she repeated, and she ran her fingertips along his jaw, which tingled from the contact with his dark gold stubble and his skin. He'd hadn't shaved; he probably hadn't had time.

He blinked away those unshed tears and stared at her as if he was trying to focus. She'd already guessed that he was exhausted earlier at Roberta's. Then he'd come home to whatever had happened here.

"Are you okay?" she asked again.

He released a ragged breath, and her face was so close to his that she felt it against her skin, against her lips, like a kiss. Startled by the sudden rush of attraction she felt, she pulled back. She hadn't felt anything like that since she was a teenager. Since Cody…

"I'm fine," he said. "It's just…like finding out something you always believed was true isn't, that something you always thought was real…"

He glanced around him suddenly, as if worried someone was eavesdropping. After catching *her* doing it a couple of times, Bethany couldn't blame him for checking.

He lowered his voice to a whisper and finished, "Like finding out Santa Claus isn't real…"

She understood his not wanting Molly to overhear him saying that. He didn't want to shatter her innocence. Was that how he felt now? Like his innocence was shattered? Or had that been shattered two decades ago when his mother died?

"All these years, you really believed that she left you?" she asked. "You never had any doubts?"

He shrugged and sighed again. "I don't know. She's been gone for so long, and I was so young when she left. I don't think I questioned anything back then. As an adult, I've been so busy…"

That was certainly evident. He had the ranch to manage, his dad, his daughter. And all those responsibilities had literally brought him to his knees. When she'd come into the kitchen and found him cleaning up that blood…

She certainly hadn't expected to find him like that. When she'd passed through the dining room, she'd noticed where something had come off the wall—some big picture or mirror. He hadn't gotten off the blood spatter, though; it was smeared across the faded wallpaper and had stained the hardwood floor.

Even little Molly hadn't bought that it was ketchup. It was *blood*. A lot of it.

She needed to check with the hospital about Don Shepard. She needed to find out what had really happened here. But there was something more important at the moment.

Cody stood up then and extended a hand to help her up. When she put hers in his, she felt a sudden rush of warmth, like a blanket wrapping around her, making her feel safe and protected. Only Cody had ever made her feel these things…and now with as heartbroken and vulnerable as he looked, she just wanted to wrap her arms around him and hold him close. She wanted to protect him from the pain he was feeling now. Unable to resist the impulse, she did that, linking her arms around his broad shoulders to hug him.

"I'm so sorry, Cody," she said softly.

Instead of accepting her comfort and sympathy, Cody stiffened, and he stepped back, out of her loose embrace. "Is this how you notify all your victims' families?" he asked, as if he was teasing. Or just trying to change the subject. He drew in a deep breath, squared his shoulders and lifted his chin with pride. The gesture reminded her of all the times he'd done that in the past, whenever anyone had brought up his mother leaving. He hadn't wanted anyone's pity then. He'd told her that on the rare occasions when he'd actually talked about his mom. He didn't seem to want her pity now either.

"It's easier to notify a victim's family when that family is a stranger," she admitted.

His lips curved into a slight smile. "Nobody's a stranger in Bear Creek."

Which meant that somebody Kim Shepard had known had probably murdered her. Someone Cody knew.

"I'll need to talk to your father, too," she warned him.

He shook his head.

"Cody—"

"I want to tell him first," he said. "And I don't think today would be a good day. Sammy said they had to sedate him for the stitches."

With the amount of blood she'd seen, she was surprised all he needed was stitches. More reason to check with the hospital. "What really happened here? How did he get cut so badly?" she asked.

"Sammy said Dad punched the mirror in the dining room," Cody said. "There were pieces of it everywhere…" He flinched. "It's no wonder he got cut so badly."

"Why would he hit the mirror?" she asked.

Cody closed his eyes, as if trying to hold in tears. "Because he didn't recognize the man in it."

Was that because of the Alzheimer's or because that man was a killer? Was Don Shepard now grappling with guilt and the disjointed memories of everything he'd done? She needed to talk to him soon before those memories slipped even farther away from him.

But she needed to talk to Cody about something else, something that had been troubling her. "You never told me he was violent," she said.

Cody shook his head. "He's not. This is the first time he's broken something like this."

"I don't mean now," she said. "When you were younger, you never told me he was violent." Technically Roberta hadn't said he'd been, but she'd seemed to allude to the man's temper, to his bitterness. Had he taken that out on his son?

Cody's brow furrowed with confusion. "That's because he wasn't…"

"But your bruises, the hurt ribs…"

He chuckled. "Those were because I was a slow learner."

She gasped with alarm that Cody was so matter-of-fact about what had happened to him. Even though she knew now how often domestic violence went unreported until it was too late, she was hurt that he'd kept this from her. She'd thought they were close, that they'd had no secrets between them. She also felt a pang of guilt that she'd missed it. But she hadn't been an investigator then and her mom and dad had sheltered her from so much of the evil in the world. Maybe that was why it both-

ered her so much now. "He used violence with you because you didn't catch on to something fast enough?"

"Not my dad. The bronco, or the bull—whatever I
was trying to ride at the time. It took me a long time
to get good, even after I joined the rodeo. Sammy can
tell you that. He saved me more than once from getting
hurt even worse."

"Sammy…" She wasn't sure she wanted to dump
this on Cody now, too. What it had taken IAEFS, the
fingerprint database, two hours to tell her.

Sammy Felton wasn't Sammy Felton. Well, he was
now since he'd legally changed his name after his release from prison twenty years ago. She glanced around
the room, at the drying blood, and she knew she had to
share this, too. For Cody and Molly's safety.

For his father's. Although Don Shepard might be the
greater danger to Cody and Molly. Was Cody telling
her the truth about his father? Or maybe just the truth
he was willing to remember? Oftentimes victims re-
pressed their memories of abuse.

Was that what Cody had done? Maybe he'd even re-
pressed his memory of the murder. She'd closed a few
cases after talking to people who'd come forward as
witnesses to murders they'd witnessed as children. As
adults, they'd finally remembered—usually in therapy—
that they'd witnessed one parent killing the other.

"What about Sammy?" Cody asked, and his long
body tensed again. "He's not a violent man either. And
he couldn't have had anything to do with my mother's
death. He'd never been to Bear Creek until he came
home with me."

She nodded in agreement. "No, he couldn't have

killed your mother," she agreed. "Because twenty years ago he was in prison for manslaughter." Unless he'd been released early, she was still checking for confirmation of his exact release date.

Cody shook his head. "No, there must be some mistake. That's not Sammy…"

"That's the other thing," she said. "The man you know as Sammy Felton isn't Sammy Felton."

"I put him on the ranch payroll, so I have copies of his social security card and his driver's license," he said. "He's Sammy Felton."

"Now," she agreed. "Twenty years ago he was Samuel Boransky. He legally changed his name after his release from prison."

He grimaced and shook his head again. "No, you got some bad information."

"I ran his prints myself—"

"When did you fingerprint Sammy?" he asked.

"I dropped something this morning and he picked it up—"

"You tricked him!" His eyes widened.

"I was doing my job," she said.

"Of course you were," he muttered. "That's all that matters to you. That's all that's ever mattered to you."

She flinched, but she couldn't deny it. She had always put her career first. But this time, with him, it was different. This was about more than closing a case. She wanted to make sure he and Molly were safe, especially after what had happened the night before. "I'm sorry, Cody. But doing my job shouldn't be a problem for anyone…unless they have something to hide. Unless they have secrets."

He lifted his hands as if she was accusing him. "I have no secrets."

"No, but it seems like a lot of them have been kept from you. A lot of secrets have been buried here at the ranch."

Chapter Fourteen

A lot of secrets have been buried here at the ranch.

Once again, even long after she'd left, Cody had Bethany's last words echoing inside his head. All these years, his mother had been buried here at the ranch. The woman he'd loved most in his life, until he'd fallen for Bethany Snow, hadn't left him. He should have been happy his mother hadn't deserted him, but he couldn't help mourning her and that he would never have the chance to see her alive again. He would only see her as he had the last time, as skeleton remains buried in a barrel.

Was that why he'd always been so drawn to that spot? Had taken Bethany there all those years ago until it became their special spot? Had he, on some level, felt closer to his mother there?

The enormity of it all sank in and he sank onto a kitchen chair. He'd been standing in the kitchen since he'd told Bethany to show herself out. It probably hadn't been that long ago, actually, because Molly had only checked on him once after she'd heard the door close.

She'd been disappointed that Miss Bethany had left

without saying goodbye to her and Snowball. But then Molly had remembered Bethany's promise to meet them later that evening in the town square. He groaned with regret over his promise to bring Molly there. He couldn't break it—even with as broken as he felt.

His mother was dead. She would never get to meet her granddaughter.

And Molly would never get to know her...

Cody didn't have many memories of his mother to share with his daughter. But maybe now, knowing the truth, he would let them come instead of suppressing them like he had over the years. Because it had been too difficult to think about her. He hadn't wanted to feel the resentment he could see his father felt over her leaving.

His dad couldn't have had anything to do with her death, no matter what Bethany believed. He'd been too broken after she'd left, too devastated. Don Shepard had loved his wife so much. They'd been high school sweethearts, like Cody and Bethany.

His dad hadn't talked about her often, but he'd told Cody that when he had started dating Bethany. His dad had warned him about falling too hard when he was that young. He'd told him that people changed...sometimes without you even realizing it.

Cody had thought then that his dad was talking about how his mother must've changed enough to leave them. But could he have been talking about himself? What had happened all those years ago that Cody's mother had wound up buried on the ranch?

A motor rumbled as a vehicle approached the house. Then it shut off and a door opened and closed with a slam. And then another. And then footsteps pounded up the

steps to the back door. Sammy pushed it open and ush-
ered Don inside in front of him. Both his father's hands
were bandaged, and there was another bandage on his
forehead, beneath some strands of gray hair that were
matted with dried blood.

"Oh, Dad!" Cody exclaimed with concern. He jumped
to his feet and rushed toward him, gripping the older
man's shoulders. He'd once seemed so broad to Cody, so
big and strong. But now he could feel the bones beneath
his hands, feel the frailty. "Are you okay?"

Don stared at him, bleary-eyed with confusion and
probably exhaustion. "What happened?"

That was what Cody wanted to know, about now
and about the past. But he wasn't the only one. Bethany
wanted to know, too, because she wanted to close another
cold case. Was that all this was to her, when to him it was
more heartbreak? He'd told her to leave before his father
got home, that it only made sense for her to question the
man when he wasn't so heavily sedated. As for Sammy...

Cody didn't know what questions she could have had
for the retired rodeo clown. It wasn't as if he could have
hurt Cody's mother, especially if Bethany was right, if
he'd been in prison when she'd disappeared.

"What happened, son?" his dad asked, and he reached
out his bandaged hands and cupped Cody's face like
Bethany had earlier. But Don's bandages were rough
against his skin while Bethany's hands had been soft and
warm. When she'd hugged him, he'd wanted to hug her
back and never let her go. He'd loved her so much once.

Like his dad had loved his mom...

Cody remembered that, remembered how they used
to dance around the kitchen. How they'd sing and laugh.

Tears stung his eyes as the memories he must have suppressed for so many years suddenly washed over him. He must have buried those memories inside his mind because it had hurt to think of those happy times and realize his dad hadn't laughed like that since his mom had disappeared, not even with Roberta.

Cody hadn't just lost his mom twenty years ago; he'd lost his dad then, too. Long before the Alzheimer's had even affected him.

"Son?" Don queried, and now he sounded more confused than concerned, as if he wasn't sure Cody was Cody.

Cody felt like that, too, like everything and everyone was so surreal. "Yes, Dad, it's me. I'm fine. I was just worried about you."

"Why?" Don asked.

"You had a little accident," Cody reminded him.

"I wrecked the truck?"

"No…"

Don nodded. "Yeah, I did. I wrecked that old plow truck…"

Cody's blood chilled. Could he mean the truck that had run Bethany off the road, the one that someone had fired that gun out the window of? While it hadn't had the plow on it, it had the carriage for one. No. His dad couldn't be talking about *that* truck. Cody shook his head. "No, you broke a mirror, Dad."

Don snorted. "Well, that's not good. That's bad luck or something, isn't it?"

"Cody here doesn't believe in luck," Sammy said. "Whenever any of the other riders would spout off some silly superstition, that's what he'd say."

"I don't believe in luck. I believe in faith," Cody murmured the words with Sammy. Somehow his friend must have sensed Cody needed the reminder. Cody did believe in God and in Heaven, and his mother was there now, watching over them.

"Your mama used to say that," Don said. Then he glanced around the kitchen. "Where is she?"

"She's gone, Dad," Cody reminded him. He considered telling him the rest—that she was dead. But then his dad staggered and nearly collapsed. And Cody wondered if he already knew.

"Let's get you into bed," Sammy said. "You've had quite the day, Don." He turned toward Cody. "You, too. And I suspect it's not over yet." He gestured toward the little girl who was running toward them through the dining room where Cody had cleaned up all the glass.

"Grandpa!" she exclaimed. "What happened?"

"He broke a mirror," Sammy said matter-of-factly.

Molly whirled toward Cody and frowned at him. "You told me it was ketchup. You lied!"

"I'm sorry, honey," Cody said. "I didn't want to scare you before I knew how badly Grandpa was hurt."

"He has a lot of stitches, but he's fine," Sammy said. "Just tired. I will get him cleaned up and into bed and then start lunch for us. Or maybe we'll make it an early dinner since it's afternoon now. We could probably all use an early night."

Molly shook her head. "No, Daddy and I are going to town," she said. "He promised I could talk to Santa tonight. That I could tell him what I want…"

Another memory suddenly rushed over Cody, of his one visit to Santa after his mom had disappeared. He'd asked Santa to bring her back, but she hadn't returned. After that, Cody hadn't returned to Santa because he'd decided Santa wasn't real. He hadn't gone back to that holiday display since—not even when Bethany had wanted to check it out when they were teenagers. He'd given her some excuse then, that he'd had to help his dad on the ranch.

Maybe she was right.

Maybe he did have secrets of his own. Like how he wished she was here with him now, holding him like she'd held him when she'd broken the news to him, the terrible news. Like how he was probably falling for her all over again even though he knew there was no hope.

Big snowflakes drifted down from a black sky sprinkled with stars that seemed to reflect the twinkling lights dangling from the branch of every tree in town square. "Your mother outdid herself this year," neighbor after neighbor told Bethany as she passed them on her way to the center of the little Christmas village.

"I don't know what we would do without your mom," another local said as Bethany passed the line of people waiting along the candy cane fence for their child's turn to talk to Santa.

Bethany smiled and nodded. She hadn't realized how much she'd taken her mother for granted all these years, but now, realizing that Cody's mom wasn't just gone but was dead… She shuddered to think of losing her mother that way or any way at all.

"Cold?" a deep voice said.

She turned to find Cody standing next to her. She'd

stopped farther down the line where she could peer over the fence at the big red sleigh parked in the very middle of the town square. She shook her head. It really wasn't that cold yet, at least not by Bear Creek or Chicago standards. There was no wind, and even though it was snowing, those big flakes melted the minute they hit the sidewalk and the shoulders of her wool jacket. "No, I'm fine. How are you?" Her heart had been aching for him since she'd left him looking so devastated in the middle of that bloody kitchen.

"I'm not cold either," he said, probably purposely taking her question literally. "But maybe that'll change soon. Molly probably asked Santa for the white Christmas she's been talking about since we moved to Montana." He uttered a weary sigh. "Hopefully that's what she asked him for."

"I'm surprised you came tonight," she said.

"I didn't want to disappoint Molly," he said.

She peered around him then. "Where is she?"

He gestured toward the sleigh where a little girl stood next to Mrs. Claus, who was helping kids into the sleigh and onto Santa's lap. "Your parents recruited her to be their elf."

She leaned over the fence and peered harder at the Clauses in their furry red suits. "That's my mom and dad?"

"You didn't know?"

When she'd returned from the ranch, she'd found a note on the kitchen counter that her mother must have scrawled on her way out the door: At the town square. And she'd just assumed her father had still been at the sheriff's office, like he had always been when she was growing up.

She shook her head. "They didn't say a word about it…"

"Then I guess you're right," Cody said. "Everybody has secrets. Even your perfect parents."

Uncertain if that was envy or resentment in his voice, she turned back to him. He looked so exhausted and pale, except for the dark circles beneath his eyes. He obviously hadn't gotten any rest since she'd left him earlier. "Are you okay?"

He nodded. "Yeah, I'd just hoped to be farther on the barn right now. But it was a pain getting the excavator out and now he hasn't been able to come back…and…" His voice got gruffer and trailed off.

She knew he wasn't really worried about the barn. Bethany reached up to touch his face like she had earlier, in his kitchen. "Cody, are you all right?"

"Yeah, I just don't want to think about it:.." He shuddered now. "To think about her."

Maybe it had been easier on him to think she'd left and was alive and happy somewhere else. Maybe that was why some victims' families got furious with her when she notified them. In the cases like Kim Shepard's, when the victim had been missing, there had been hope that they might still be alive. Bethany's notification extinguished that hope. "I'm sorry."

"I know you have to investigate—"

"You should want me to," she pointed out. "Don't you want to know the truth? Don't you want justice for what happened to her?" Other families had been consumed with the need for their loved ones' killers to be caught.

"Is it going to bring her back?" he asked.

"It'll bring you closure," she said.

He snorted. "I had closure," he said. "I'd accepted long ago that she just took off with that ranch hand. But now that she's been dug up, it's digging up all this…" He clutched his fist against his chest, as if his heart ached.

Maybe that was how it felt. "Do you want to go somewhere?" she asked. "Do you want to talk? Mom and Dad will keep an eye on Molly…"

His brow furrowed, pushing up the brim of his black hat. "Are you asking as an old friend or an FBI agent trying to solve a case?"

"It's not just a case to me," she admitted. It couldn't be with how she'd once felt about him, with how she still felt about him.

"I don't know what you want from me, Bethany."

That was fair. She didn't know either. She knew what he wanted, or at least what he didn't want: *her*. He didn't want her in his life or in Molly's. She could understand that he wouldn't want his daughter hurt when she left.

"This was a mistake…" She shouldn't have come down to the town square. She shouldn't have accepted Molly's invitation to join them. The last thing she wanted was to make Cody's life any more difficult than it was. "I'm sorry."

She needed to leave before Molly spotted her. She whirled away from the candy cane fence and headed back down the sidewalk. People called out to her, like they had earlier. But she ignored them now. She already felt like a fool for not knowing her parents were Santa and Mrs. Claus, that her mother didn't just take care of her dad and her own family but of every other family in town.

How could she investigate Cody's mother's murder when she wasn't even aware of everything that was happening in her own family? She still didn't know why her dad had been acting so strangely since he'd picked her up from the airport. She didn't know if he was really okay.

He never would have taken the time to help out her mom like he was now. He'd rarely gone to church with her before, but now he was sitting in a sleigh wearing a Santa suit. Sure, he was getting older, but he couldn't have mellowed that much naturally. At least she didn't think so.

Was he sick?

Like that day at the excavation site, she was reminded again of a snow globe: this one of a town square decorated for the holidays with the snow drifting down over it and the town and the people and Bethany trapped inside the glass with someone watching her.

This was more than the curious stares of the people she passed. This was more intense than that, more focused... so much so that a chill raced down her spine. Like someone was staring at her.

It was probably Cody. She glanced back over her shoulder, but she didn't see him following her. She didn't see anyone following her, but she suddenly felt pursued, like someone was chasing after her. She quickened her pace. She'd walked to the town square, and it hadn't felt far from the house when she'd headed down.

But now as she headed back, she felt like she was miles away from home rather than just a couple of blocks.

She felt as if she would never get there. She started to jog, the soles of her boots pounding against the concrete. She was nearly there.

She just had to cross one more street.

She looked both ways before stepping off the curb. But she didn't see it…until it headed straight toward her, the big truck with just one light on the front of it.

The engine revved as the driver stomped on the accelerator. And she was frozen, too stunned to move… to save herself…

The single light on high beam illuminated Bethany Snow's pale face as she stood frozen directly in front of the truck. There was such shock and disbelief on her face, as if she couldn't believe it was going to end like this. That this was how she was going to die.

The FBI agent had to die. Because she was the one who would ultimately uncover all the secrets. Who would learn the truth…

That could not happen.

There were some secrets that needed to stay buried forever…the way Bethany Snow was going to get buried before Christmas.

Chapter Fifteen

Cody didn't know what compelled him to suddenly run to catch up to Bethany. Maybe it was that she hadn't given him an answer. She hadn't told him what she really wanted.

Could she want him again?

Could she still have feelings for him like he had for her?

Did it matter, though? They had even less of a chance of making a relationship work now than they'd had when they were teenagers. Since he knew where she was headed, he hurried to catch up with her. So he was close when she stepped off the curb to cross the last street before her house.

He was close enough that he saw the truck pull away from the curb, flash on its single light and accelerate as it headed directly toward her. He was there when she froze in front of it.

But he didn't freeze. He jumped into the street and pushed her out of the way. Cody had so much momentum that he pushed her all the way across the street and down onto the sidewalk. And he went with her, falling on top of her and out of the way of that speeding truck.

The truck swerved and the brakes squealed as it slowed just enough to career around the corner. Once it was gone, he drew a deep breath into his burning lungs. He'd stopped breathing when he'd seen her standing there about to get hit.

He eased back and stared down at her. Her eyes were open, but she looked dazed. He must have hurt her when he'd knocked her down with such force. "Are you okay?" he asked, his voice gruff with concern. "Did you hit your head?"

He touched her then, running his fingers through her silky hair, looking for blood or a bump or something.

And finally she released a shaky breath, as if she'd been holding it for a long while. "No. I'm fine. I just…"

"It was close," Cody said. Much too close…

"I froze," she admitted, her voice sharp with self-recrimination. "You saved my life, Cody. Thank you." She lifted her head and pressed her mouth to his.

It was the briefest of kisses but it jolted him to his core, to his heart.

"See, I told you that you had to kiss Snow White," a little voice said.

Panic shot through Cody again. He rolled off Bethany and jumped up from the sidewalk. Had his daughter followed him? Had she been that close to the truck?

"Molly!" he gasped.

But she wasn't alone. Mr. and Mrs. Claus accompanied her.

Sheriff Snow rushed forward and helped his daughter up. "We shut the sleigh down for the night and were just walking back to the house with Molly. What happened? Did you get hit?" He looked as shaken as Bethany was.

"Thanks to Cody, I didn't get hit. It was *that* truck. And before you ask, I didn't get a look at the driver. And I should have." She shook her head.

"Somebody tried to hit you?" Molly asked with alarm, and she shoved between Bethany and her father to hug her.

Bethany patted her shoulders. "I'm sure it was an accident," she assured the little girl. "Like maybe their brakes weren't working or something."

Cody smiled at her in appreciation that she was trying not to scare his daughter. Cody was scared enough for both of them. Bethany could have been killed. He could have been killed. He was surprised Bethany hadn't yelled at him like she had last night when he'd followed her into danger.

"Are you okay?" Molly asked with concern.

Bethany leaned down and pressed a kiss to Molly's forehead. "You are so sweet. And yes, I am, thanks to your daddy. He saved me."

Molly whirled toward him. "You did, Daddy?"

He shrugged.

"He did," Bethany insisted.

"You are a prince then, Daddy," she said. "You saved her with a kiss."

Sheriff Snow chuckled. "I'm not sure that's what did it." Then he focused on Cody, and the smile left his face. "Did you see anything?" he asked.

"It was a black truck. A heavy duty Ford. Plow carriage and that missing light. I didn't see the plate or the driver." He shrugged. "I'm sorry."

The sheriff reached out and squeezed his shoulder. "You did good, son. You're both okay. That's all that matters."

But it wasn't. Not with that truck and driver out there somewhere, just waiting for another opportunity to try again. Bethany wasn't safe.

Neither was he. And not just from the driver...

His lips tingled yet from that contact with hers. He was falling for her again. Or maybe those feelings he'd already had for her were unburying themselves...just like all the secrets.

As she watched Cody and Molly drive away from the town square, Bethany had the feeling he hadn't told her something. That there was something he was holding back from her. A secret he claimed not to have.

She was keeping a secret from him, too. She'd run away from him because she hadn't wanted to admit to her feelings for him...even to herself. But then that truck had nearly run her down, certainly would have run her down if not for Cody pushing her out of the way, and her feelings of gratitude had been so intense she'd had to express them. With that kiss...

It had been brief, but it had opened up her heart to feelings she hadn't let herself feel for so long. She'd fought hard to close herself off to that kind of love. All those years ago she'd been scared that she would lose herself to loving him like she'd thought her mom had lost herself. But now she wondered if her mom was always who she was going to be. *Everything.*

Mom had her arm around Bethany's shoulders now, and she turned her away from the street to head back to their house. Bethany and her father had let Cody leave to take his daughter home and because there was no point calling the state troopers again. They hadn't found the truck last time, and it was already long gone again now.

Where? And who had been driving it?

After Molly and her mom and dad had joined Bethany and Cody on the sidewalk, other people had rushed up to check on them. But nobody had been able to help identify who'd been driving the truck.

That was just one of Bethany's frustrations at the moment. She was more concerned about her other feelings, the feelings for Cody Shepard that were overwhelming her. She'd worked so hard to steel her heart, to stop herself from falling for anyone, from letting anyone interfere with the life she'd planned for herself. Even Cody all those years ago…

But he was older now and even more special than the boy she'd known back then. He was a man now. A father. A hero.

He'd saved her life. That was the only reason she'd kissed him, out of gratitude. No. She was lying to herself if that was all she'd thought it was. It was more than that. He was more than that.

He had always been.

She wasn't just emotionally shaken; she was beginning to physically shake in reaction as well. She was glad when they arrived at their house.

"Are you really okay?" her mother asked when she guided her through the kitchen door her father held open for her.

Bethany shook her head as tears stung her eyes. But she blinked them back. "It's just been a tough day, Mom."

"You told him?" her father asked.

She nodded.

"What?" Sally asked her husband. "What are you talking about?"

"We identified the remains uncovered on his ranch," Bethany said. "It was his mom."

Sally gasped. "Oh, no…that poor woman…" She pressed a hand against her heart. "All these years everyone has talked about her, spreading such horrible gossip about her, thinking such uncharitable thoughts about her running off with some ranch hand, and nobody knew the truth."

But somebody had. The person who'd killed her.

"The ranch hand…" Bethany began. "Whatever happened to him?"

"The gossips always claimed that he disappeared the same time Kim Shepard did," her father remarked.

Had he disappeared like Kim Shepard had? Six feet under? Or thousands of miles away to escape a murder charge? Maybe Kim had refused to leave her husband and child for him, and he'd given her no choice. "Do you remember his name?" she asked, eager to have another suspect besides Cody's dad.

Her dad shook his head. "You'll have to ask Cody or his dad."

"Poor Cody," her mother said.

"How did he take it?" her father asked.

Bethany suspected his mind had gone where hers had, to thinking that maybe Cody had known, that maybe he'd witnessed the murder. As a lawman, Mike Shepard would look first at the spouse as the primary suspect. "Cody was shocked. Or so he seemed…"

Her mother's brow furrowed beneath her red Santa hat. "What do you mean? I'm sure he *was* shocked."

"But he showed up in town tonight," her father pointed out. "And he seemed fine."

"He was probably just putting on a brave front for his daughter," her mother said. "That's what parents do."

For the second time that night a chill chased down Bethany's spine. "Is that what you two are doing? Is there something you're keeping from me?"

When Mr. and Mrs. Claus shot each other a significant look, she knew she was right. "Come on," she said. "You really think you can keep something from me? I'm a trained investigator." Not that she'd been acting much like one since her return to Bear Creek. She'd been acting more like a lovestruck teenager, unable to think clearly. Or at least to act quickly.

She couldn't believe she'd frozen in the street like she had. If not for Cody, she would have been run down for certain. She shivered in response.

"You're cold," her mother said. "Let me make some hot chocolate for all of us." She turned toward the stove, but Bethany caught her hand and felt her fingers shaking. She pulled her mother around to face her. "What is it?" she asked.

Her mother shook her head. "It's really nothing for you to worry about."

Bethany looked from her mom to her dad again. He looked even paler than usual and older and thinner. "What's going on?" she asked him. "Are you two getting a divorce or something?" She was teasing because it was easier to bring up that unlikely possibility than to ask if her father was sick like she really suspected.

But maybe she shouldn't joke about what seemed to be a thing now, couples divorcing when they were older and empty nesters. Her parents had been empty nesters for twelve years. It had to be something else; something maybe even worse…

Her father slid his arm around his wife and shook his head. "No, thank God. But I'm lucky she didn't divorce me long ago for how absent I've always been." He kissed Sally's cheek. "She's a saint, just like everyone claims."

Her mother blushed.

Heat rushed to Bethany's face, too, but she wasn't embarrassed over their affection for each other. She was embarrassed that she'd often thought the same thing—that her mother should have divorced her father.

"I wished I would have appreciated your mother more," he said.

Oh, God. Was Mom the one who was sick?

Bethany tightened her grasp on her mom's hand. "What is it? I'm not four years old like Molly Shepard. Tell me what's going on."

"It's not as bad as you're thinking," her father said. "It really was the wake-up call I needed to realize how I'd been living, or not living."

"What are you talking about?" she asked, her head beginning to throb. Maybe she had hit it on the sidewalk, or maybe she was just too exhausted to follow what he was saying. Or not saying.

"Your father had a stroke a few months ago," her mother said.

Despite her suspicion, Bethany gasped with shock. Now concern and fear gripped her. "Oh, my God. Why didn't you call me? Why didn't you tell me?"

"It wasn't a big one," her father said. "I got to the hospital in time for them to stop any lasting damage."

She released a shaky breath. "That's good. But still you should have called…"

"You were in the middle of that big case," her mother reminded her.

"Did you tell Diana or Bill?" she wondered.

Her mother shook her head. "Diana's so busy with the kids. And Bill was in the middle of moving to his new parish."

Tears rushed to Bethany's eyes. "So you dealt with it all on your own?" She hated how nobody had been there for the woman who was always there for everyone else. Especially her children…

"Your mother is the strongest person I know," her father said. "She handled everything, told the office I had a flu bug and needed a week off—"

"A week!" Bethany exclaimed. "You had a stroke!"

"I know," her father said. "But it wasn't bad."

"But what caused it?"

Her father sighed. "High blood pressure. High cholesterol. Stress. Genetics…" He shrugged. "I'm a mess."

That was why he looked so much older than she remembered him being.

"Not anymore," her mother said. "You're getting healthy, and when you retire—"

Bethany snorted. "Like that will ever happen."

"New Year's," her father said. "I've already given my notice, and the mayor and the town council have started a quiet search for an acting sheriff to serve out my term until the next election."

She narrowed her eyes and shook her head. "This

town never does anything quietly. And nobody has mentioned a word about your retiring. The mayor and the town council must not think you're actually going to do it. Frankly, neither do I."

He grinned. "Then you're all wrong. While the call I had with the stroke wasn't as close as the one you probably had tonight with that truck, it was the wake-up call I needed. I know what's important. It's not a job, Beth." He tightened his arm around his wife's shoulders and hugged her close to his side. "It's your mother. Our family. And my faith."

With his words, Bethany froze again in shock like she'd had in front of that truck. Something was barreling down on her again—feelings. But it had been a long day, and she was too exhausted to deal with them now...or to even fully acknowledge them.

Her father didn't miss like the truck had. "You need to think about what's truly important to you, Beth."

"You and Mom, of course," she said.

"Is that why you haven't been home in all these years?" he asked.

"I've been busy..."

He sighed and nodded. "I understand that. Here it's small-scale, tickets and petty thefts. For you, it's always another murder to solve. But you know what, Beth? If you don't work those cases, someone else will. It's not like you're personally letting criminals go free if you choose to do something else."

"That promotion..." she murmured.

"Have you accepted it yet?" her mother asked, and she suddenly appeared tense...with dread? Obviously her mother didn't want her to take it.

She shook her head. "Not yet."

"Why not?" her father asked.

She shrugged. "I don't know. I had time to think about it before I had to accept, so I'm taking that time."

"Take it," her father urged. "Take your time and think long and hard about what will make you really happy, Beth."

She stared at him in confusion. "I don't understand. You've seemed so proud of me, of that promotion. You've been bragging to the mayor, to everyone."

"I am proud of you," he said. "You've done wonderful things with your life. And I'm sure you'll do a lot more. Whether or not you take that promotion is up to you, and I'll be proud of you no matter what you decide. I just want you to think about some other options."

"What other options?" she asked. "Staying in Chicago?"

"Moving home," he said. "Taking my job."

"What?" The thought had never crossed her mind. It was an option she'd never considered. And with that option came other ones...like Cody.

Maybe. If he would give her another chance.

He had given her one tonight—when he'd saved her life. If she didn't catch whoever had been driving that truck, though, she might not have the time her father was urging her to take.

She might not have any options but one: death.

Chapter Sixteen

A few days had passed since that nightmare day Cody had learned the body uncovered on the ranch was his mother's. Excavation had resumed at the site today. He needed to head there, but after dropping Molly at preschool, he'd headed home first.

A few days had also passed since his father's injuries, and the sedation had worn off long ago. But Bethany hadn't questioned him yet…because when she'd called two days ago to set up a time to talk to Don, Cody had admitted he hadn't told him yet.

He hadn't talked to Sammy about what she'd told him either. When she'd again called this morning, he'd used the excuse of being busy. But they both knew the truth: that he didn't want to know the truth. Not when it came to the men he'd loved and trusted most in his life. Maybe he already knew the truth; they were the good men he believed they were. When Bethany had called those couple of days ago, she'd asked about another man as well as his father and Sammy. She'd asked about Tom Campbell.

Well, she hadn't known his name, but when she'd wanted to know the identity of the ranch hand his mother had supposedly run off with, Cody had told her. And his shoulders had lifted with relief. Tom Campbell. He had to be the one who'd killed his mother. But then who had been driving that truck…?

Was Tom Campbell back in Bear Creek? Or had he actually never left?

Now that he'd dropped off Molly, Cody could talk freely to his dad and Sammy without her overhearing anything. He pulled his truck up beside Sammy's and shut off the ignition. Before he could lose his nerve again, he jumped out and headed up the porch steps to the back door. When he stepped inside, the smell of cinnamon and nutmeg greeted him, and for a moment he felt like he was in Mrs. Snow's kitchen, not his own.

There weren't any signs left of the blood. Sammy had done a better job of cleaning it up than he had.

"Baking?" he asked Sammy.

The older man turned away from the stove. "Just making oatmeal for your dad," he said. "It's his favorite."

"You take such good care of him," Cody said. "Of all of us…" He couldn't believe what Bethany had learned about him. It had to be wrong. "And I think of all the times you saved my life while I was riding. All the other lives you saved…" Sammy had knocked him out of the way of a rampaging bull countless times—like Cody had done a few nights ago with Bethany and that truck.

Sammy released a heavy sigh and dropped onto one of the kitchen chairs. "I thought you knew…" he mumbled, "since that day she dropped her sunglasses."

"What?"

"Your FBI girlfriend," Sammy said. "I was pretty sure she used the ploy to get my prints."

And yet he'd given her back her sunglasses, he'd let her walk away with evidence of his… Of his what? His true identity? His past?

Cody dropped onto one of the chairs across the table from Sammy and he released his own sigh.

"Do you want me to leave?" Sammy asked.

"I want you to explain," Cody said. "Tell me what happened. Tell me who you are."

"You know who I am, Cody," Sammy said. "I'm your friend. I would do anything for you. For your dad. For your daughter."

Tears stung Cody's eyes as he worried. Had Sammy been driving that truck? Was he the one who'd tried to hurt Bethany? And why? Did he think that Don Shepard had murdered his wife? Had his father admitted something to his caregiver that he hadn't told his son? Had Sammy been trying to protect him?

"Who's Samuel Boransky?" he asked.

Sammy blew out a ragged breath. "A stupid kid who didn't know his own strength and was too proud and hotheaded to walk away from a fight."

"Ah, Sammy." While Cody felt for his friend, he was also relieved. Samuel Boransky didn't sound all that different from Sammy Felton. "So it was just a bar fight?"

"Just?" Sammy shook his head. "It was more than that. It was years of pent-up frustration, of being called trash and taking abuse at home from my stepdad and half brother and knowing that everything everybody said about me was probably true, that I was no good just like my dad and my brother."

Cody reached across the table then and gripped his friend's shoulder. "Sammy, you're the best man I know—next to my father and Sheriff Snow. You're a good man—" He would have said more but his phone vibrated in his pocket. He ignored it, figuring that it was probably Bethany calling to say her interviews couldn't wait any longer. She had to close her case.

"Take it," Sammy said. "It's probably your Agent Snow."

"She can wait—"

"She's waited long enough," Sammy said. "I'll wake your dad up. We can talk to him before she gets here." He stood up then and rushed out of the room.

Cody grabbed his phone from his pocket. He'd already missed the call, but it hadn't been from Bethany. It was from the excavator again. He hit redial to return Bruce's call. "What's up?"

"You tell me. How many bodies you got buried around this place?"

"What?" Cody asked. "You found another one?"

"Yup, but it actually wasn't buried. Somebody had tossed it into that old well. I'd taken the lid off it and shone my light in it to see if the water was still there…" His voice trailed off, gruff with emotion or revulsion. He cleared his throat and continued, "I already called the sheriff's office. Snow and his daughter are on their way."

The old well…

How many times had he and Bethany sat on the lid of that thing and talked about their future? Had that body been there then? They'd never lifted the cover. They'd never checked. "That's good," Cody said.

"Nope, there's nothing good about this. Even I can

tell this one was murdered. Bullet hole in his skull. And I want nothing to do with it, Cody. I'm pulling my stuff out of here. You're going to have to find another excavator. This place has already given me nightmares." Then he disconnected the call.

The excavator hadn't been the only one having nightmares. Despite how tired he was, Cody had barely slept since the first body was found. Building the barn was the least of his worries right now. What if this newly discovered body belonged to the person who'd disappeared the same time his mother had? If it was Tom Campbell, then he probably hadn't killed Cody's mother, which meant that someone else had killed them both.

Even I can tell this one was murdered...

It was only a matter of time before Bethany got here from the crime scene, only a matter of time before she came to question his father. Cody didn't have to be an FBI agent to know the spouse being cheated on was the one who oftentimes snapped and killed the cheating couple. Was that what had happened all those years ago? Had Kim Shepard been fooling around with the ranch hand like people had said? Cody wanted to talk to his dad. He wanted the truth—if his father even knew what it was anymore.

He pushed himself up from the table and headed through the living room to his father's suite at the back of the house. Roberta had had it built when she'd moved in because she'd wanted a main-floor suite. Cody had figured she just hadn't wanted to sleep in the room where his mother had.

The door was shut, and when Cody reached for the knob, Sammy called out, "Don't come in here, Cody."

But Cody was already turning the knob, already pushing open the door…and like the day that truck window had rolled down, the barrel of a gun pointed in his direction. This time Bethany Snow wasn't here to knock him out of the way.

Bethany had already been on her way to the ranch when the excavator's call had come into dispatch. So not much time had passed since his call when she drove the sheriff's department SUV onto the scene.

"That was fast," Bruce Willard said from where he stood in front of a mound of dirt. It was twice as high as what had been there from his previous dig. The barn Cody was building was a big one. Bruce walked away from that toward the old well. "I'm glad it's you," he said. "I thought it was just the sheriff when you pulled in."

"My dad's on his way," she said. He'd taken off shortly after she had.

"This is more a case for you," Bruce said. "You're the one with the experience with the cold cases. And this one looks as cold as the last…" He pointed toward a skeleton that had been wrapped in plastic. The blade of the backhoe must have ripped some of it, or Bruce had. The skull was visible with a hole in the middle of the forehead.

"The back of the skull is just about gone but there's a bullet rolling around inside what's left of it…" He shuddered.

Definitely sounded like he'd ripped that plastic. "Where did you find it?" she asked since it wasn't near the hole.

"In the well," Bruce replied with a jerk of his thumb. "I probably shouldn't have pulled it up…"

He shouldn't have, but she wasn't going to chastise him with as shaken as he seemed. She crouched down to inspect what Bruce had found. The plastic was wrapped so tightly around the body it had just about mummified some of it and kept the clothes pretty intact as well. It would be easier to determine the identity of this victim, especially since it looked like a wallet was sticking out of what was left of a shirt pocket. Using her phone she snapped a couple of pictures of it, then she rolled on some plastic gloves, reached inside the opening Bruce had ripped, pulled out that wallet and flipped it open. It was stuffed with wads of what looked like cash and a driver's license for Thomas Samuel Campbell.

It was a Nevada license. Not a Montana one. And the address listed on it was one she'd seen recently…on the old records she'd pulled up for Samuel Boransky. At one time these two men had lived in the same place. Why?

What was the man who called himself Sammy Felton to Tom Campbell?

Loved one or killer?

When she'd initially read his sentence, she'd figured he was in prison when Kim Shepard had disappeared. But now she'd confirmed he'd been released early due to good behavior. The timeline would have been tight, but it was possible he'd made it from prison to Bear Creek just about the time Kim Shepard and Tom Campbell had been murdered.

She needed to call Cody, needed to warn him to get away from the man. Now.

"Beth!" her father shouted, and she whirled around

to find him rushing up from his idling SUV. "There's been a call about a gunshot wound at the ranch. An ambulance is on its way."

That was what Bruce had said when he'd called: that this person had died from a gunshot wound. But why would an ambulance have been dispatched? She pointed toward the bones. "I don't think anyone's going to be able to save him."

"Up at the house, Beth," her dad said. "There's been a shooting up at the house."

Panic gripped her. She was too late. Somebody had been hurt.

Cody?

Molly?

She ran toward the SUV. "We have to hurry!" she shouted, panic making her pulse pound frantically. "The ambulance is going to take too long to get there. We have to do whatever we can."

"Let's pray then," her father said as he directed her toward the passenger's side of his SUV. "Let's pray."

"Please, God," she choked out through her tears. "Please God, don't let anything happen to Cody or Molly."

"Molly's with your mom," her dad said. "At preschool. She's fine. She's safe."

Her breath shuddered out with relief.

"The gunshot victim is a male."

"Please, God, please not Cody…"

She'd lost him once through her own fault, because she hadn't been able to see what was most important. And while she'd had a close call the other night, it hadn't given her the clarity her father's close call had given him.

It was this—Cody having another close call, or

worse—that made Bethany finally realize what was most important to her.

Him. Molly. Family.

And faith. "Please, God…"

Chapter Seventeen

There was blood.

So much blood…

Cody couldn't get it to stop even with the towels he had pressed against the wound. Where was the ambulance?

"Please, God, send help," Cody prayed.

Sammy reached up and grasped Cody's wrist, and his grip was surprisingly strong despite how much blood he'd already lost through the hole the bullet had put in his belly. "It's okay. I'm going to be okay…"

"Yes, you are," Cody said. He could hear the sirens now. "Hang on."

"I'm not going anywhere," Sammy said. "I owe you. I owe you and your dad…"

"For what?" Cody asked. His dad had just shot him. Of course he hadn't meant to; he couldn't have meant to do that. He'd just been having such a bad episode, had been so confused.

"For Tom…" Sammy whispered.

"What do you mean? What are you saying?"

But Sammy's grasp loosened, and his hand dropped back to the floor where he lay in Don Shepard's bedroom. "No!" Cody cried. He couldn't be dead.

Footsteps pounded on the hardwood floors as help finally arrived. But was it already too late?

"Cody!" Bethany gasped, and she dropped to her knees beside him. "Are you all right? What happened?"

"My dad found a gun somewhere and was waving it around. He didn't know what he was doing. I don't think he even knew what it was, he's so out of it today…" His voice cracked with the emotions overwhelming him. "Sammy saved me. Help him…" He could not lose his best friend. He couldn't.

Bethany felt Sammy's neck and said, "He has a pulse. He's still alive."

"Where's the ambulance?" he asked.

"They're just pulling in," she assured him. "My dad will bring them right back." She gazed around the room then. "Where's the gun? Did you get it away from your dad?"

"Sammy got it away from him," Cody said. And if he hadn't, Cody might have been the one lying on the floor in a pool of blood.

Don Shepard sat on his bed with his arms wrapped around himself, rocking back and forth. He was so out of it, slipping further and further away from reality.

"Has he been hit, too?" she asked.

Cody shook his head. "No…"

"Where's the gun?"

Cody couldn't move, couldn't even straighten his arms as he continued pressing those towels against Sammy's wound. "It's under the bed," he told her.

Bethany leaned forward and pulled the revolver out from under the bed then checked the magazine and the chamber almost as if it was instinct for her. "It's empty."

"Now…" Cody said. Then he heard more footsteps and yelled, "Back here! Hurry!"

Within seconds the paramedics were there, treating Sammy on the floor before sliding the stretcher beneath him and carrying him off. Cody wanted to jump up, wanted to chase after them, but he was shaking too badly. When he lurched to his feet, Bethany was there, grasping his arm—maybe for support, maybe to keep him from leaving.

"We need to talk about what happened," she said. "First off, why in the world do you have an unsecured gun in your house with your dad and your daughter?" She flinched as if horrified about what could have happened.

What had happened was bad enough. What could have happened…

He refused to let his mind go there, refused to even imagine that it had been Molly who was hurt. As it was, he couldn't stop shaking, couldn't stop worrying about Sammy.

"I didn't have any guns in the house," he said.

She lifted the empty gun she held in her other hand, confusion all over her face.

He had no idea where that one came from, where it had been. How could he have missed it? "I went through the house when we first moved in and checked for guns," he said. "There was only one in the house, an old hunting rifle that I locked up in the barn. My dad never owned a revolver. There's no way that gun was in the house."

"Well, obviously it is now," she said. "Tell me exactly what happened." She glanced at his dad again then back to him. "Did Sammy attack you?"

He gasped. "Sammy saved my life. He came in here to wake up Dad, and I got the call from Bruce about the body." He cringed as he remembered that call. "I came back here to talk to Dad, but Sammy told me not to come in…"

"But you did anyways." She either assumed or knew him too well.

He nodded. "Dad had the gun, but he didn't know what he was doing, maybe even what it was, but he pointed it toward the door when I opened it. He was so out of it that I don't think he knew who I was. Maybe he thought I was an intruder or that Sammy was. Before my dad could shoot me, Sammy grabbed for the gun." He shuddered. "He took the bullet that could have…"

Her grasp on his arm tightened. "I prayed. I prayed so hard…"

"Keep praying," he said. "Pray for Sammy. I can't lose him. He's my best friend."

"I think he has something to do with Tom Campbell," she said. "That might be why he's here."

Cody shook his head. "No, he's here because he knew I needed help. He's here because he's my friend. He has nothing to do with Tom Campbell."

"Tom Campbell?" Don asked, raising his head at the mention of the guy's name. "He was no good."

Cody's blood chilled as he remembered Sammy's re-action when Dad had said something along those lines, of having a feeling Tom was no good. Had Sammy re-acted that way just because Dad had used the phrase Sammy said had been directed at him so many times? Or had he known Tom?

"I found Tom Campbell's Nevada license on that body Bruce just found," she said. "He and Samuel Boransky once resided at the same address."

"No good," Don muttered again. "Just like that brother of his in prison for murder."

Panic gripped Cody, and he shook his head. Was Tom the half brother Sammy had mentioned? "No…" Surely he would have told him, but then he hadn't told him anything about his past until today.

"Mr. Shepard," Bethany said, and she stepped closer to the bed.

His dad turned toward her and smiled. Unlike ear-lier, he looked completely lucid now. "You're the sher-iff's daughter…"

She nodded.

"You broke my son's heart, just like I warned him you would."

She released a shaky breath and nodded. "I broke my heart, too," she told him. "But that was all a long time ago. I'm all grown up now, and I work for the FBI."

He smiled again. "Always were an ambitious girl… trying to prove you were just as smart and strong as your daddy to get his attention."

A gasp rang out and Cody turned to find her dad standing in the doorway.

Bethany ignored them both as she focused on his dad. "Did you have this gun or did Sammy?" she asked.

Cody was used to answering for his father who often

didn't remember anything. Maybe Bethany hadn't had much experience with people with Alzheimer's, so she didn't understand how fleeting his lucid moments were. Too fleeting for Cody to keep him home any longer? After this shooting, he might not have a choice. "Dad had the gun," he told her again.

"I found it," Don said. "I found it in the old plow truck."

Cody had been running the ranch for just a few months now. He hadn't had a chance to go over all the equipment yet. So he didn't know what the plow truck looked like, just that the ranch would have one. Could it be an old black Ford?

"Where's the old plow truck?" Bethany asked him.

"Behind the hay barn where it always is."

Cody furrowed his brow. He would have noticed the truck that had nearly struck Bethany if it was anywhere on the property. He'd even looked behind that barn recently, when he'd been trying to find Sammy and Dad. "I haven't seen it. There's no truck back there." But then it wouldn't have been there if it had been running Bethany off the road.

His father looked at him like he'd lost his mind. "It is now."

Bethany turned toward her father. "Dad, can you take this gun into custody? And look for that old plow truck? I want to get to the hospital to talk to Sammy whatever his name is…"

"Felton," Cody said. "That's who he is now."

"Beth," her father said. "Remember your prayers." He gestured at Cody. "They were answered. Don't take that for granted." Then he took the gun from her and turned and headed out of the room.

"What was he talking about?" Cody wondered.

She shook her head. "I can't get into that now. It has to wait a little longer."

"What has to wait?" he asked.

But she ignored his question and started out of the room. With a glance back at his father to make sure he was all right, he headed after her. She was in a hurry; she'd already made it onto the front porch. "Beth!" he called out to her. "What is it?"

"I'll talk to you later," she said. "We're close to wrapping this up now. To finding out who killed your mom and Tom Campbell and who's tried to kill us."

He shook his head again. "No, we're not. Not if you think it's Sammy. You yourself said he was in prison when my mom disappeared."

"He should have been," she said. "But he was released early for good behavior. It has to be Sammy. Don't you see?"

He shook his head. "No, I don't." And he wouldn't. "Sammy's not a bad man." He'd just proven that—by taking a bullet for him. And by being so careful not to hurt his dad when he'd taken that gun from him. That was how Sammy had wound up getting shot instead of anyone else.

"He did time in prison."

"For a bar fight that got out of hand."

"Somebody died."

Sammy might be dying himself. Cody needed to get to the hospital, too. But he had his dad to worry about. While he could leave him alone in his room, he couldn't leave him alone in the house. But he didn't want Bethany questioning Sammy when his friend needed to focus on recovering. "You always think the worst of everyone, Bethany. You accused my dad of beating me earlier this week, and he's never laid a hand on me. He's barely ever raised his voice to me. He's not a violent man."

"That mirror…"

"That was an accident," Cody said.

"Looks like it wasn't the only one…" a deep voice announced as the sheriff walked back from the direction of the barn. "*That* truck, with the broken headlamp, is parked back there."

Shock flooded Cody. "I don't know how to explain that…how to explain any of that."

"There's only one explanation," Bethany said. "Sammy."

But Cody just couldn't believe it. "He's a good man, Bethany, just like my dad is a good man. You have to have faith in people. You have to stop thinking the worst of everyone just because of all the horrors you've seen in your job. You have to have faith." And he had to hang onto that faith himself. He knew Sammy; he'd trusted the man with his daughter, with his father and now with his own life. It couldn't be him.

"I do," she said. She ran back up the steps to press her lips to his. "I have faith." But that was all she said before she jumped into the sheriff's SUV and sped off, leaving her father standing on the porch with Cody.

"What's going on?" he asked.

"I think she's going after her man," her dad said.

"She's got the wrong one."

* * *

Bethany was halfway to town before she realized she was wrong. And Cody was right.

Sammy had taken a bullet for him. He wouldn't have done that if he'd been trying to kill him. He wouldn't have done that if he was out for revenge or to protect himself.

And Cody's dad. Cody's dad had seemed so simple and earnest. Like he'd been every time she'd visited the ranch...

Like Cody had said, she couldn't even remember him ever raising his voice. So why had Roberta alluded to him being violent...?

Her hands gripped the wheel as it suddenly occurred to her why Roberta had said what she had. And instead of continuing on to the hospital, Bethany turned the wheel and headed toward the veterinarian she'd always admired so much, to the woman she'd idolized.

The parking lot was empty but for a muddy pickup that must have belonged to Roberta. A sign on the door said the practice had closed early that day, but when Bethany turned the handle, the unlocked door opened.

The receptionist wasn't behind the desk, but Roberta was. When she stood, Bethany wasn't surprised she had a gun in her hand. An old hunting rifle. Had she taken that from the Shepard Ranch like the plow truck?

"As much as I've always admired you, I seriously underestimated you," Bethany realized.

"I haven't underestimated you," Roberta said. "I knew, sooner or later, you'd figure it out."

"That's why you've been trying to kill me," she said.

Roberta nodded. "It's why I'm going to kill you now..."

Bethany realized she'd made her second mistake in coming alone to confront the older woman. A small-town killer was every bit as dangerous as a big-city serial killer. Maybe even more so because they had more to lose when the truth came out, so they were even more determined and desperate to protect themselves.

Her other mistake had been in thinking that she had time to tell Cody how she felt. That she loved him.

Because Roberta already had that shotgun cocked and Bethany wasn't certain she could draw her gun from where she'd tucked it into the back of her jeans in time to hit the vet first.

Chapter Eighteen

"She's wrong," Cody told Bethany's dad the minute her SUV pulled out of the driveway. "It's not Sammy."

The sheriff shrugged. "It all adds up."

Cody shook his head. "But it doesn't. The night she was run off the road, I looked behind the barn, I looked all over the ranch for my dad and Sammy, and that truck wasn't there then. In fact I haven't seen it until today—"

"My wife took it," a male voice chimed in, and he turned to find his dad standing in the doorway. "My wife took it. That's where I found that gun, in the glove box. I didn't know there was a bullet in it."

This moment of lucidity for Cody's dad was lasting longer than it usually did, as if he knew how important it was that he explain what happened. Maybe he knew he could be taken from the ranch if he didn't.

"What?" Cody asked. "What wife?"

"Your stepmother," he said. "Your mother's gone."

Cody drew in a deep breath and said what he should have told his dad days ago. "She's dead. We found her body on the ranch. Hers and Tom Campbell's."

"He had a thing for your mother, kept trying to sweet talk her…" He sighed. "Something I never took the time to do. I should have taken the time…"

"She didn't leave the ranch," Cody assured him. "She didn't leave us…" His voice cracked with emotion.

"Roberta said that she did…that your mother told her she didn't love me anymore."

"Mom was friends with Roberta?"

"They talked…when she came out to the ranch for the animals. Roberta talked to Tom, too." His brow furrowed then as if he was figuring out what Cody was starting to as well.

Had Roberta orchestrated everything? But why…

Then Cody remembered how often the vet had come around the ranch. And he realized now that it hadn't been just for the animals. She must have always had a thing for his dad. Even when he'd been married?

"Do you think…" Cody began, and he turned toward Mike Snow. Then he remembered what she'd said that day she'd been treating Snowball, and he widened his eyes with the sudden shock of it.

"What?" the sheriff asked.

"She knew about the shooting at your house," Cody said.

Mike Snow snorted. "Small-town gossip, everybody heard about it…"

"But who else would have known that the person had shot at me?" Cody asked. But for the person who'd aimed that gun…

"I'll call in the state police," Sheriff Snow said. "I'll send them over to pick her up." He was already pulling out his phone.

"Stay with my dad!" Cody shouted as he headed toward his truck. He had to hear it from her…from this woman who'd claimed to love his father, to love him.

But yet he'd never let himself get that close to her. Maybe he'd worried that she'd take off someday like his mother had. Or maybe on some level he'd suspected…

A short while later, he realized he wasn't the only one. The sheriff's SUV was already in the lot of Roberta Kline's veterinarian practice, and when he walked up to the door, which had been left partially open, he could hear them talking.

"You should understand," Roberta was telling Bethany. "You know you can achieve anything if you work hard enough."

"You worked hard for Don Shepard," Bethany said. "You killed his wife."

"Tom Campbell killed her," Roberta said. "I paid him to do it."

"I found the money in his wallet. It'll probably have your prints on it," Bethany said. "You know you're not going to get away with this."

As he peered through the door, he could see Bethany had a gun clasped behind her back, her body turned toward the side so Roberta couldn't see it. Roberta stood behind the reception desk, a shotgun against her shoulder. His heart pounded hard with fear and panic. He had no idea what to do…or if he'd only get in the way if he tried to intervene.

"I knew that the minute I heard your father had asked you to investigate," Roberta said. "I heard all those news reports about you, how you caught that killer who'd gone for years with no one ever suspecting him. That was me.

No one ever suspected me…" Then she uttered a ragged sigh. "No, not no one. I think Don had some doubts."

"Is that why you tried framing him?" Bethany asked. "Using his truck? Saying that he was violent?"

"As violent as a fly." Roberta snorted. "He didn't even like to kill those. He's a good man. A great rancher who really cares about his animals. That's how I fell for him, working at the ranch with him. But I knew he'd never leave Kim. They were so in love. So I had to get rid of her. And then when Tom Campbell refused to leave town unless I paid him more money, I had to get rid of him, too."

Cody must have made some noise because Roberta turned toward him with the gun.

And a blast rang out.

The shot went wide. Roberta's. Not Bethany's. Her bullet struck Roberta's shoulder and knocked her back. Roberta's shot had missed Bethany by a lot, striking the doorjamb of the door behind her instead. Bethany jumped over the reception desk and grabbed the shotgun from the floor. More concerned about the woman grabbing another weapon than her wound, she rolled Roberta onto her stomach and cuffed her arms behind her back—all the while Roberta screamed.

Bethany didn't know if it was with pain or frustration. When she turned back toward the door and saw Cody leaning against the jamb, Bethany let out a small scream of her own. "I didn't know you were there!" she exclaimed. "Are you all right?" She jumped back over the desk to rush to his side. Blood seeped through his shirt. Roberta wasn't the only one who'd been hit in the shoulder. She pulled out her cell, but before she could even call it, police cars sped into the parking lot.

And an ambulance.

"I'm not hurt," Cody said.

But she suspected he was just in shock and couldn't feel the pain yet. Just the stinging. She'd been shot once and knew how it felt. And how much more it would hurt later.

"Sweetheart, we need to get you to the hospital," she said, and she slid her arm around his waist, helping him out to the lot, toward the ambulance.

"You said that's where you were going," he reminded her.

"Then I realized you were right," she said. "You were right about everything. Even all those years ago when you said we had something special. Something worth fighting for…"

"I said that?" he asked.

"Yes, and I should have listened. I should have tried. But I loved you so much I thought I would lose myself… like I thought my mom…" She groaned with frustration. "I was wrong about everything. My dad is right. That's what I decided on the way to your house when we didn't know if you'd been shot or not."

"What did you decide?" he asked.

"I'm going to turn down that promotion."

"You are? Why?" he asked.

"Because I had a better offer."

"But I haven't even proposed yet."

She smiled as love filled her heart. "Yet…"

"Well, first I have to hear about this better offer."

"Sheriff," she said. "I'm going be acting sheriff of

Bear Creek when my dad retires on New Year's Day. I'll run for the position at the next election." And if her mother helped her campaign like she'd always helped her dad, there was no way Bethany could lose. "So you're just going to have to get used to me sticking around town."

"You don't want to leave?"

"Never," she said. "I realized what's important. You. Molly. My family. My faith." She blinked back the tears stinging her eyes. "You're what matters most. I love you, Cody Shepard. I always have. And I know that I always will."

"Then marry me," he said. "I've had the ring for twelve years. Marry me."

Before she could say yes, he slumped against her as his knees gave out and he passed out cold. Maybe from blood loss, maybe from shock. Or maybe the shock had finally receded enough for him to feel the pain.

"Hurry!" she shouted at the paramedics as they rushed toward them with a gurney. She wasn't worried that he was hurt very seriously. The only blood she'd seen on him was on his shoulder. But she wanted him to get treated quickly. She wanted him well and happy for Molly, for Christmas and for their wedding.

Epilogue

"I never been up this late before," Molly murmured sleepily as she leaned against Bethany's side where they stood at the front of the church. It was almost midnight.

They were waiting until 12:01 to say "I do," to be pronounced man and wife. They'd waited twelve years, but Bethany had been determined to start the new year as Cody's wife, as Molly's mother…as the acting sheriff of Bear Creek.

She wouldn't work the hours her father had, though. She would always be there for her family and for the man she loved with all her heart. He stood next to her in front of the minister with his best man at his side. Sammy was a strong man. Despite his abdomen injuries, he'd insisted on being released from the hospital so that he could be there for Cody, as he'd always been.

He'd admitted that the last time he'd talked to Tom, Tom had mentioned Bear Creek and making some money by charming a woman named Shepard into leaving town with him. So Sammy had always suspected his brother had been the reason Kim Shepard disappeared, but he hadn't been sure if he'd actually charmed her or killed her. That was why he'd befriended Cody in the beginning, to find out more and to try to make up for what his brother had cost him. He was a good man, like Cody had always known. But Cody—he was the best.

The bells began to chime in the tower, jerking Molly awake. "Here's the ring!" she called with excitement. She handed over the wedding band that Don had miraculously remembered he'd kept all these years, after he'd found it in the yard where he'd tossed it. Roberta had had Tom take the ring from Kim as proof he'd killed her. Then she'd left it for Don to find after she'd packed up all of Kim's other belongings to make him believe his wife had left him. But Kim wouldn't have left him and Cody any more than she would have taken off her wedding band while she was alive. Now neither would Bethany.

Cody slid the gold band over her knuckle up against the diamond engagement ring he'd bought for her so long ago, with money he'd saved up from working on the ranch. He'd had it in his pocket that night she'd dumped him. It was beautiful. And so was he and their daughter.

"I love you so much," he said. "Always have and always will."

"I now pronounce you man and wife," the pastor declared.

"You need to kiss her, Daddy," Molly said. "Just like the prince kissed Snow White."

* * * * *

**Inspired by true events,
The Secret Society of Salzburg
is a gripping and heart-wrenching story of
two very different women united to bring
light to the darkest days of World War II.**

Don't miss this thrilling and uplifting page-turner
from bestselling author

RENEE RYAN

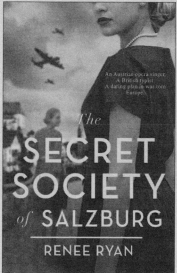

"A gripping, emotional story of courage and strength,
filled with extraordinary characters."
—*New York Times* bestselling author **RaeAnne Thayne**

Available now from Love Inspired!

LOVE INSPIRED
LoveInspired.com

Get 4 FREE REWARDS!

We'll send you 2 FREE Books plus 2 FREE Mystery Gifts.

FREE
Value Over
$20

Both the **Love Inspired®** and **Love Inspired® Suspense** series feature compelling novels filled with inspirational romance, faith, forgiveness and hope.

YES! Please send me 2 FREE novels from the Love Inspired or Love Inspired Suspense series and my 2 FREE gifts (gifts are worth about $10 retail). After receiving them, if I don't wish to receive any more books, I can return the shipping statement marked "cancel." If I don't cancel, I will receive 6 brand-new Love Inspired Larger-Print books or Love Inspired Suspense Larger-Print books every month and be billed just $6.49 each in the U.S. or $6.74 each in Canada. That is a savings of at least 16% off the cover price. It's quite a bargain! Shipping and handling is just 50¢ per book in the U.S. and $1.25 per book in Canada.* I understand that accepting the 2 free books and gifts places me under no obligation to buy anything. I can always return a shipment and cancel at any time by calling the number below. The free books and gifts are mine to keep no matter what I decide.

Choose one: ☐ **Love Inspired**
Larger-Print
(122/322 IDN GRHK)

☐ **Love Inspired Suspense**
Larger-Print
(107/307 IDN GRHK)

Name (please print)

Address   Apt. #

City   State/Province   Zip/Postal Code

Email: Please check this box ☐ if you would like to receive newsletters and promotional emails from Harlequin Enterprises ULC and its affiliates. You can unsubscribe anytime.

Mail to the **Harlequin Reader Service:**
IN U.S.A.: P.O. Box 1341, Buffalo, NY 14240-8531
IN CANADA: P.O. Box 603, Fort Erie, Ontario L2A 5X3

Want to try 2 free books from another series? Call 1-800-873-8635 or visit www.ReaderService.com.

LIRLIS22R3

Get 4 FREE REWARDS!

We'll send you 2 FREE Books plus 2 FREE Mystery Gifts.

FREE Value Over **$20**

Both the **Harlequin® Special Edition** and **Harlequin® Heartwarming™** series feature compelling novels filled with stories of love and strength where the bonds of friendship, family and community unite.

YES! Please send me 2 FREE novels from the Harlequin Special Edition or Harlequin Heartwarming series and my 2 FREE gifts (gifts are worth about $10 retail). After receiving them, if I don't wish to receive any more books, I can return the shipping statement marked "cancel." If I don't cancel, I will receive 6 brand-new Harlequin Special Edition books every month and be billed just $5.49 each in the U.S. or $6.24 each in Canada, a savings of at least 12% off the cover price, or 4 brand-new Harlequin Heartwarming Larger-Print books every month and be billed just $6.24 each in the U.S. or $6.74 each in Canada, a savings of at least 19% off the cover price. It's quite a bargain! Shipping and handling is just 50¢ per book in the U.S. and $1.25 per book in Canada.* I understand that accepting the 2 free books and gifts places me under no obligation to buy anything. I can always return a shipment and cancel at any time by calling the number below. The free books and gifts are mine to keep no matter what I decide.

Choose one: ☐ **Harlequin Special Edition**
(235/335 HDN GRJV)

☐ **Harlequin Heartwarming Larger-Print**
(161/361 HDN GRJV)

Name (please print)

Address _____ Apt. #

City _____ State/Province _____ Zip/Postal Code

Email: Please check this box ☐ if you would like to receive newsletters and promotional emails from Harlequin Enterprises ULC and its affiliates. You can unsubscribe anytime.

Mail to the **Harlequin Reader Service:**
IN U.S.A.: P.O. Box 1341, Buffalo, NY 14240-8531
IN CANADA: P.O. Box 603, Fort Erie, Ontario L2A 5X3

Want to try 2 free books from another series! Call 1-800-873-8635 or visit www.ReaderService.com.

*Terms and prices subject to change without notice. Prices do not include sales taxes, which will be charged (if applicable) based on your state or country of residence. Canadian residents will be charged applicable taxes. Offer not valid in Quebec. This offer is limited to one order per household. Books received may not be as shown. Not valid for current subscribers to the Harlequin Special Edition or Harlequin Heartwarming series. All orders subject to approval. Credit or debit balances in a customer's account(s) may be offset by any other outstanding balance owed by or to the customer. Please allow 4 to 6 weeks for delivery. Offer available while quantities last.

Your Privacy—Your information is being collected by Harlequin Enterprises ULC, operating as Harlequin Reader Service. For a complete summary of the information we collect, how we use this information and to whom it is disclosed, please visit our privacy notice located at corporate.harlequin.com/privacy-notice. From time to time we may also exchange your personal information with reputable third parties. If you wish to opt out of this sharing of your personal information, please visit readerservice.com/consumerschoice or call 1-800-873-8635. **Notice to California Residents**—Under California law, you have specific rights to control and access your data. For more information on these rights and how to exercise them, visit corporate.harlequin.com/california-privacy.

HSEHW22R3

HARLEQUIN
PLUS

Try the best multimedia subscription service for romance readers like you!

Read, Watch and Play.

Experience the easiest way to get the romance content you crave.

Start your **FREE TRIAL** at
<u>www.harlequinplus.com/freetrial</u>.